Side Piece Chronicles:

3

Delilah's Revenge

Joi Miner

Side Piece Chronicles 3
Book 3 of Side Piece Chronicles Series
Copyright © 2016 Joi Miner
Published By: Southern Goddess Ink

Synopsis

In the final episode of Side Piece Chronicles...

Delilah's back!!! And she's got a score to settle. After spending ninety days in jail, she's out for blood! Blaming Sheila for ruining her life, she devises a plan to get revenge on the entire Price family – Sheila, Tyrone, and Tammy. But her plans are derailed when her past comes to find her.

Sheila, Tammy, and Tyrone just want to go on with their lives and forget they ever knew Delilah. Their plan to open the Mojo Lounge is coming through and soon they will take the Gump by storm. But Delilah isn't making it easy. She shakes the very foundation their happily ever after is built on and she won't let up until someone is dead or she's back in jail.

Will Delilah get to see her enemy's blood spill? Or will the Prices to get away with their lives and sanity, and erase Delilah from their lives forever?

This entire series is dedicated to
Ashley Foster aka Ghetto Angel
Look boo! I did it!
Three books, based in our hometown in your honor!
I know you've been watching me grind this book out and smiling.
My angel! Love you! Always!!

March 19, 1987 – September 13, 2015

Contents

Synopsis..3

Prologue..7

Sheila...9

Ron...12

Tammy..14

Tyrone..16

Sheila..18

Delilah...20

Ron...22

Anthony..26

Beth..29

Samantha..31

Delilah...34

Tanisha...38

Sheila..41

Anthony...44

Ron..46

Tammy...48

Tyrone..50

Sheila..55

Samantha..58

Anthony...62

Tyrone..64

Delilah...68

Tre...72

Tammy...76

Tanisha...78

Sheila..81

Tyrone..83

Anthony...88

Samantha 91
Ron 93
Tre 96
Tyrone 101
Beth 105
Delilah 107
Anthony 111
Sheila 115
Tre 122
Beth 126
Delilah 130
Ron 132
Tyrone 139
Tammy 146
Anthony 152
Samantha 156
Delilah 161
Epilogue 163

Prologue

Sheila

Two months earlier...

"Miss Price," Dr. Kingston said, looking at my chart before looking at me.

"Yes?" I answered nervously.

Ron reached over and grabbed my hand. I'd had to tell him about my possible cancer diagnosis when things got serious with us. The first time we'd had sex had been so painful that I'd had to make him stop. So when I scheduled my appointment at the Cancer Center and could actually get the tests run, he'd been hell-bent on coming with me. This was the follow-up appointment and I would be getting my results today.

I squeezed his hand because I knew the results couldn't be good. As much as he tried to keep his professional face on, the doctor's eyes told that there was something wrong.

"Ahem," he cleared his throat before continuing, "You have ovarian cancer. Stage two. It appears to be very aggressive and, in the time that we had to wait for you to heal from your previous surgery, it has progressed extensively. We need to begin treatment immediately if we want to slow it down and cure it before it spreads to other places."

I sat there like a deer in headlights, speechless. I felt numb. I couldn't cry. Couldn't scream. Couldn't pinch myself and wake-up from this nightmare. This shit was real and having an abortion after fuckin' with Anthony's trifling ass had almost cost me my life! I was still frozen in shock when Ron spoke up.

"So, Dr. Kingston, what happens now?"

"We want to begin chemotherapy immediately, along with radiation. We usually do the chemo treatment in cycles. I recommend every twenty-one days to give your body time to rest and recover. If we don't begin to see results after three cycles, we'll remove the ovary. Right now, it only appears to be in the left one so you will still be able to have children with a little help and planning."

I was hearing him but it wasn't registering. Thoughts of murdering Anthony were running through my mind until I realized that if he hadn't gotten me pregnant, I may not have found out about the cancer as soon as I did. I wasn't scheduled for my annual for another eight months. The cancer could have spread and been fatal by then.

"So when do we start?" I finally asked, my mouth dry.

"Let's begin with the oral chemotherapy and we'll schedule your first cycle of radiation for next week."

"Ok," I said, sadly. I felt like I was about to pass out.

He wrote my prescription and left. We walked to the front desk to schedule my radiation. Ron had to support the majority of my weight because my legs felt like they were made of Jell-O.

The ride to the pharmacy and home were a blur. When we got there, Tammy, Tyrone, and my mom, Tanisha were sitting there waiting to hear the outcome. I just wanted to lay down so I asked Ron to fill them in. I heard my mom holler out to God and then whimpering and crying. I rolled over and went to sleep. I'd face them after I had the chance to rest and collect my thoughts.

Sheila

"Ron stop," I said, giggling, "We're supposed to be workin'. The grand opening is less than two weeks away!"

"I *am* workin'," he said, still kissing on my neck. "I'm workin' on getting you to put that damn laptop down so I can clock some hours in these sheets."

I sucked my teeth, pretending to be annoyed, but I was loving every second of it. We'd been inseparable since our first date. He was more than I could have imagined he'd be. From being by my side through chemo to helping me surprise Tyrone and Tammy when they got back from their honeymoon by having all of their furniture moved into their new home, he was ready and willing to help with anything that I needed. I wasn't used to being treated this well, but I was definitely getting used to it.

I pushed him away playfully and tried to bring his attention back to planning for the promotion of the Mojo Lounge.

"So, Thursday is the VIP soiree. We got DJ Shadow spinnin', an open bar, and fully catered dinner with waitress service that night. That one is unadvertised and by invitation only so we gotta make sure the swag bags are on point. Then Friday, we've got the actual grand opening party. How your street team been doin' gettin' the word out? How are the presale tickets movin'?"

I'd been working from the house since my cancer diagnosis. During the day, Shawn came here and used my home office. We'd forwarded all of my calls to my business phone so I only went in the office for urgent meetings. I was so grateful that everyone had been willing to work with me. Both of my moms, brother, Jeff, and Tammy waited on me hand and foot. It was awesome but sometimes the shit got annoying. My favorite nights were the ones, like tonight, when Ron ran everyone else off and he and I sat up planning. But tonight, for some reason, he was terribly distracted.

"We're almost out of flyers and have about forty or fifty of the presale tickets left," he said, sighing and sitting back against the headboard of my bed.

"That's phenomenal, bae! Y'all have really sold two hundred tickets?" I beamed.

"Well, I'm good at what I do," he said, winking at me. "I got the models ready and Crown Royal Black s a title sponsor with free shots all night."

"This is gonna be the hottest black-out party the Gump has ever seen," I said, excited. "I really couldn't have pulled this off without you, baby. I love you."

"Well, I accept payment in the form of kisses and that thing you do with your hips," he smirked.

"Focus, bae. We're almost done," I said unable to hide my smile.

"Then we've got the Family Fun Fest in the courtyard on Saturday with the scavenger hunt inside sponsored by Kayla's Rentals. That's gonna be a full-on carnival," he pointed out.

"Wait, who'd you get to spin Friday night?" I interrupted him, trying to get all of the details.

"DJ Meek," he said, smiling because he knew she was my top choice.

"Noooooo! You did *not* get Meek!" I yelled. "How the hell did you pull that one off? She's usually booked *months* in advance."

"It took some persuading because that one there is 'bout her business. She's almost bad as you, Nel," he said, shaking his head. "I started working on her after our first meeting."

"Really? Awww," I said leaning over to kiss him passionately. "Do you think we could get her on payroll?" I grinned.

"Baby steps, baby. Baby steps," he said, pulling my laptop out of my lap. "Now it's time for you to get some rest. You've got radiation in the morning and I've got a meeting with another model, Danielle, tomorrow after I get you home and in the bed. Did you email the list to me and Shawn of what you needed done for the rest of the week since you're not gonna be able to work?"

"Yes, bae," I said, rolling my eyes. I loved how he took care of me but hated feeling helpless. I was so ready for this shit to be over.

I reached over and turned the lamp off before cuddling up against him. He let out a pained grunt as I felt him getting hard behind me. I knew he wanted to have sex but we couldn't the night before I had radiation. He was so patient and I felt terrible. I settled in my mind that he was worth me stepping outside my comfort zone.

I rolled over and looked into his eyes. The moonlight shining through my blinds illuminated the room just enough for me to be able to see those soft browns staring back at me.

"Baby, thank you for being here for me. I love you so much," I said, staring into his eyes.

"I love you, too, Nel," he said, trying to hide the pain and longing that he was feeling.

"You know, this is the first time you actually said it back," I pointed out.

"I didn't think I needed to say it," he said, his forehead wrinkling.

"You're right," I said, mischievously, "actions speak louder than words."

I pulled back the covers and reached down, pulling his dick out of his boxers. I massaged it, looking at him lovingly. He leaned in to kiss me and I shook my head 'no'.

If I'm gonna do it, I might as well go ahead before I lose my nerve, I thought to myself.

I sat up, making a beeline for his waist. I opened my mouth and wrapped my full lips around his dick. The feel of it in my mouth made me wanna gag. When I got that feeling, though, I thought of everything he'd done for me. All the days he'd spent working with Shawn to get my shit done. Picking Jeff up from school. Helping with Tammy and Tyrone's house. Everything. Down to him bringing a microwave to the park on our first date.

Unlike Anthony, I didn't have to worry about Ron cheating on me. I felt like we were actually building something. He was with me almost every day, spending the night several times a week. I thought of all these things while I mimicked the porn stars we'd watched together.

I could feel him tensing up. I must have been doing something right. I sucked and slurped all over his dick, loving the sound of him moaning every time his dick hit the back of my throat, making me gag a little. He got really hard in my mouth and I knew he was about to cum. I decided that it was go hard or go home so I prepared for him to squirt into my mouth.

Grabbing the sheets, he moaned loudly as I felt his dick start to throb and a warm wetness shot into my mouth. I closed my eyes tightly and swallowed.

When I looked up at him, I saw him staring back at me with a look of gratitude and disbelief on his face. I laid back down, pulling the covers back up over us and settled in to go to sleep.

"I thought you didn't do that," he whispered in my ear, wrapping his arms around me.

"I don't. Never had anyone I felt was worth it," I confessed.

"Woman, I love you!" he said, resting his chin on top of my head.

I dozed off, smiling. I was really getting my chance to see what real happiness felt like.

Ron

After I got Sheila settled and checked in with Shawn, I drove down Vaughn Road towards Mugshots. I was meeting my new potential model for lunch. She'd missed the deadline but when she sent me her portfolio, I decided to meet with her and give her a shot. I got there early and ordered a beer and an order of sweet potato fries while I waited.

I knew her as soon as she walked in. She was beautiful with mocha brown skin and her hair braided up into micros that hung almost to her waist. Her body was *bad* and she wasn't scared to show off her C-cup breasts and toned abs in her V-neck crop top. Her fitted jeans hugged her hips tightly. Her legs were hella long, lengthened even more by her open-toed stiletto heels. I stood from my seat and waved her over to the table. Her walk was mesmerizing, like she was moving to her own rhythm. When she reached the table, I caught a glimpse of her perfect ass. Her jeans had it in a bear hug.

"Danielle, nice to meet you," I said, extending my hand.

"Nice to meet you, too," she said as we sat down and the server brought my fries and beer and took Danielle's order.

"So, I wanted to meet with you to discuss your modeling submission. As you know, the deadline has passed..."

"I'm aware. I decided to give it a shot anyway because I'm passionate about my modeling," she said, interrupting me. "I know that working with someone of your caliber would look great on my resume but, and this is the most important thing, I feel that it'll be a learning experience. I'm in my thirties but I'm never too old to learn, especially from a pro like yourself," Danielle said, laying it on thick.

I leaned back in my chair, beer in hand, and sized her up. There was something about her that I wasn't really feelin'. I couldn't put my finger on it, but it was something. On the other hand, my dick was jumpin' because she was sexy as hell. It didn't help that Sheila was out of commission because of her chemo and radiation. Even though she'd never given head before and had changed that for me, I wanted to feel some pussy. Danielle sat, studying me and stealing a few of my fries, waiting for my response. The smirk in her eyes felt like she was reading my mind. I snapped out of it.

"I'm not really a fan of flattery, but in this case, it'll get you in the door. But you're gonna have to catch up to the girls who are already working. Can you sell fifty pre-sale tickets in the next two weeks?" I challenged her.

She smirked again. I could tell she was cocky and that her words were just words. She wanted to make some money and a name for herself. I knew an opportunist when I saw one. But opportunists had been my biggest moneymakers in the past. You just had to remind them, every now and then, who's in charge.

"I sure can," she said, leaning forward so I could get a full view of her breasts. I diverted my eyes, making her smile even harder. She was playing a game with me and I had a feeling, if I didn't watch myself, I'd be on the losing end of it.

After she filled out and signed the contract, I handed her the tickets. I was racking my brain trying to come up with a reason to leave ASAP. Gratefully, my phone started to ring. It was Sheila. When her face popped up on the screen and "Coffee" by Miguel started playing, I smiled. I saw a hint of something come across Danielle's face but I just figured it was frustration with being interrupted. I answered the phone.

"Hey baby... you okay? Ok, I'll be there in just a few minutes. I'm finishing up my meeting right now... Love you, too."

I ended the call and stood from my seat. I put a fifty on the table to cover my fries and beer and Danielle's food.

"You have my business line. Hit it if you need anything. There'll be a model meeting day after tomorrow at seven in the evening at Vantech Marketing. You'll receive an email with details by this evening. Welcome to the crew, Danielle," I said, extending my hand.

She sat there with her arms crossed across her chest, pouting. I shrugged and walked off. I had to get to my baby. I didn't have time to deal with an employee throwing a damn temper tantrum.

Tammy

I sat in the bathroom in disbelief. Tyrone had gone back to work and I was in the last couple of weeks of physical therapy before I went back to the plant. I'd enjoyed playing Susie Homemaker but I was ready to get out of this damn house and back to doing something productive.

But now, I wasn't sure how long I was gonna be able to work. I stared at the positive pregnancy test sitting on my sink. I wasn't supposed to be able to get pregnant. My head was pounding and my heart was racing. I knew that because of my issues, I needed to call a doctor immediately so that I could make sure the baby would be fine.

I sat there on the toilet with my head in my hands, debating whether or not I should tell Tyrone that I was pregnant until I knew for sure that everything was fine. I decided against it. I didn't want to get his hopes up just to dash them. Especially after Samantha's spiteful ass had killed his twins because we'd gotten married. He was still hurt from that.

I wanted to tell Sheila but her ass couldn't hold water. So I was gonna have to keep this secret to myself. Placing my hands on my stomach, I began to cry. All these years I thought I would be childless. All this time with Tre cumming in me and nothing happened. But *now* I was pregnant. For my husband. The love of my life. And I couldn't tell him.

Forcing myself to get up, I called and made an appointment for the morning. I'd heard that once you got past the first trimester, there was a better chance of the baby surviving. I just needed to make it three months. Just three months.

*****

"Mrs. Price," Amelia, the cute nurse said, walking into the exam room as I lay on the table waiting.

"Yes," I answered.

"Your test results show that you are, indeed pregnant. Twelve weeks," she said, smiling.

"Twelve?" I asked, doing the math in my head and grateful that there was no way in hell the baby was Tre's.

"Yes, ma'am. Doctor Peña will be in shortly to speak with you. Sit tight."

I sat down, my palms beginning to sweat. All I wanted to know was that my baby was ok.

The doctor came in wheeling a machine with a screen in with him. I remembered it from Nel's pregnancy and smiled because I knew that he was about to give me an ultrasound. I was pretty sure he was just checking to make sure the baby was alright because it was too early to tell what I was having. I'd been spending every spare moment last night online researching everything that I could about pregnancy.

"Mrs. Price, I'm Dr. Peña. I want to check on your little one to make sure everything is alright and then I want to go over a few things with you, ok?"

"Sure," I agreed, laying back as he lifted my gown and squirted some cold goop on my stomach.

When he put the stick on my stomach, my heart skipped a beat. I heard swooshing and then the steady thump of a heartbeat.

"That's good. He has a strong heartbeat," Dr. Peña said, smiling and moving the stick around some more. "Ah, there he is."

I looked over at the screen and saw my baby. It was moving around slowly, making me think of its father and how chill Tyrone was. I couldn't hide my excitement as my tears began to stream down my cheeks. I blinked them away as the doctor snapped a few shots of my baby, our baby, for me to take with me. He turned the monitor off and gave me a napkin to wipe off my stomach.

"So, how are you feeling?" Dr. Peña asked me, looking over my chart.

"I'm great. I haven't had any morning sickness and the only reason I even took the pregnancy test was because I hadn't seen a period in months. I didn't expect it to be positive because I was told that I couldn't have children."

"Well, you were told wrong," the doctor laughed. "You're carrying a very healthy child and I don't see any issues at this stage. I do want to monitor your pregnancy very closely though, just to make sure."

"Yes sir," I said, beaming.

"You can get dressed," he instructed as he got up to give me privacy. "Oh, would you like to know what you're having?" he asked over his shoulder, a smirk on his face.

"I thought it was too early to tell."

"You're far enough along for us to be able to tell from your blood test."

"Then, no. Not right now. Can you put it in an envelope and I'll open it a little later?" I asked, in total shock.

"Absolutely," he said, walking out, "it will be waiting for you at the receptionist's desk."

I smiled from ear to ear, getting dressed. I couldn't believe the way my day was going. I was ready to get home and plan how I was going to tell Tyrone the good news!

I walked out of the doctor's office and to my car on cloud nine. When I opened my door, the hair on the back of my neck stood up. I looked around because I felt like someone was watchin' me. I didn't see anyone but I knew that something wasn't right. I shrugged it off and went home. Checking my rearview mirror all the way.

Tyrone

"Tammy! Babe!" I yelled, walking into the house after work. I took off my shoes at the door and walked through the house looking for my wife. She was nowhere to be found.

I picked up my phone to call her and then I noticed a note on the fridge.

Tyrone,

I have a surprise for you. Meet me at our spot. Room 325. See you there.

Love you,

Tammy

I smiled at the thought that she had a surprise for me but found it odd that she wanted to meet at a hotel when we were married and had a home of our own. We didn't have to sneak around anymore. Curiosity got the best of me and I hopped in the shower and got dressed. I was going to make the best of this getaway that my wife had planned for us.

About an hour later, I was walking into the Drury Inn. Getting onto the elevator, I pressed the button for the third floor. My mind was in a million places wondering what I was walking into. I knocked on the door.

"Who is it?" I heard Tammy's voice on the other side of the door.

"Mr. Price. I was told that I could find my wife here," I joked.

The door opened and as I walked into the room, I saw blue streamers and banners all over the room. There were little footprint cutouts dangling from the ceiling and a cardboard stork standing by the bed holding a baby in a handkerchief. It read, "It's A Boy". I turned to my wife standing with her back pressed against the door. She had tears in her eyes but they were contradicted by the smile on her face.

"Seriously?" I asked.

"Seriously," she said, nodding.

I ran over and scooped her up off the ground. I held her close and kissed her entire face from her forehead to her lips. I lingered in her mouth before carrying her to the bed and laying her down gently. I was filled with so much love for my wife I just wanted to be one with her.

Pulling up her skirt, I buried my face in her lap, pleasuring her until she shuddered uncontrollably. I slid off my pants and eased myself into her. I knew that I couldn't hurt the baby, but it didn't hurt to be cautious. As I stroked her, I looked deep into her eyes. I wasn't only making love to the woman I had been in love with for years, but she was now my wife, and having my child. Life couldn't get much better than this!

Sheila

"Who the fuck keeps calling my phone!!!" I yelled into my empty house, frustrated as hell because I kept getting restricted calls.

I'd called Ron and he was on his way home. I wasn't feeling well and these unwanted calls weren't helping. I leaned over and threw up into the trash can that was sitting on the side of the bed. Whoever was calling was saying they were fuckin my man. That he wasn't at a business meeting and soon my sick ass was gonna be alone again. I heard the alarm chime.

As soon as Ron walked into the room, I lit into his ass.

"Who the hell are you fuckin', Ron?" I yelled, my voice cracking from exhaustion.

"Nel baby, what are you talkin' about?" he asked, completely caught off-guard by my accusations.

"You fuckin' heard me. Your bitch has been playing on my phone and says that you were fuckin' her and lyin' to me about being at a damn business meeting."

"Nel..."

"Don't Nel me! Answer my motherfuckin' question. I don't have time for this shit. I'm sick and you leave me to go fuck another bitch?" I cried.

Ron looked at me like I had two heads. He stood in the doorway like this couldn't be happening. He came and sat at the edge of the bed before speaking.

"Have I given you any reason to doubt my loyalty to you? I know you've been in some fucked up relationships, but you ain't gone sit here and accuse me of some shit because you got some fuckin' phone calls. Get your damn head on straight, Sheila. You on some bullshit right now," he said through clenched teeth.

"Fuck you, Ron! You ain't shit! Ain't none of y'all shit. I hope that hoe was worth it. Get the fuck out!" I yelled, pointing towards the door.

"Nel..."

"Don't Nel me, nigga! Get. The. FUCK. Out!"

"Fine. You on one right now. I'll give you some space and when you get your shit together, you know my number."

He turned and walked out the same way he came. I heard the alarm chime and knew that he was gone. In a matter of seconds, I felt stupid. I tried to call him but he didn't answer. I knew Ron wasn't the type to do no dumb shit like that. But here I was dumping my baggage on him. I tried to call Tammy and her phone went straight to voicemail. So did Tyrone's. My mom answered but told me that she was at work and would have to call me back. I had to sit, alone, and feel the results of my overreaction. I'd acted on emotions and now I was gonna pay for it. I leaned over and threw up again. I knew it was gonna be a long night. I just hoped I could get someone to come help me because I'd run off my help.

Delilah

As soon as Ron left me at the restaurant, I started calling Sheila's phone. I'd heard that she was battling cancer and knew it would be easy to upset her. And it worked. After my sixth call, I could hear the frustration in her voice. That bitch had no idea what I had in store for her. And I was gonna use her man to do it all because he had no idea who I was. He thought I was some thirsty ass model chick named Danielle and I was gonna keep it that way. I picked up my phone to call Beth.

"Hey baby, everything going as planned?" I asked, walking out of Mugshots and hopping into my car.

"Yep. Anthony is at the bail bondsman's office now. They should be out in no time. And..." she paused like she had some real news, "he trailed Tammy to the doctor's office and then to the Drury Inn. Fuckin' with their heads is gonna be child's play, baby!"

I felt my face getting hot. These bitches thought they were gonna live happily ever after and I was just gonna be left by the wayside. But I had something for all their asses, Sheila, Sam, *and* Tammy. Hell, Beth and Anthony were gonna get theirs, too. They thought I was gonna let them fuckin in my house while I was locked up slide. But I had something for their asses, too. Anthony beeped in on the other line.

"I'll call you right back, baby. This is Kris," I said, clicking over before she could say another word.

"What's up?" I asked Kris, skipping the pleasantries.

"They'll be out in a few hours. Did Beth tell you I followed Tammy? She went to Party City and bought all kinds of 'It's a Boy' baby announcement shit before she went to the hotel. I think she might be pregnant."

I sucked my teeth and bit my jaw so that I didn't let my anger show. I wanted to go stomp that baby out of that bitch. But I knew that the plan that I had for her would be much worse.

"Make sure you give them the money and make it clear what they're supposed to do. We don't need no mistakes and no loose ends. Make it clear that they asses need to skip town once this shit is done. Tell 'em their lives depend on it," I explained.

"Alright," Kris said, hesitantly. "Delilah, you sure you wanna do all this? You taking shit kinda far. Especially if Tammy is pregnant."

"Nigga, I don't need no weakness in this. Your hands are all over this, so you can get with it or your ass can go to jail once it's done. Your choice," I threatened.

"Whatever, Delilah," Kris said, angrily. "Crazy bitch," I heard him whisper under his breath.

I hung up the phone without saying another word. I knew that he was gonna be a liability so I made a mental note to make sure and get enough of his DNA to plant. Nobody was gonna get in my way. I felt my face twitch. I was ready for war.

Ron

Sheila had lost her rabbit ass mind. Coming to me like I did something to her because somebody called her damn phone with some bullshit. She got a baby daddy and that married nigga she used to deal with, whose event she's still promoting, and she automatically thinks that the bullshit was coming from me. I care for her but ain't nobody got time for that bullshit. I got moves to make. I was pulled from my thoughts by my phone ringing.

"Hello?" I answered, annoyed.

"Ooh, who got you turned up to a million?" the voice said laughingly on the phone.

"Man, whatever. Who is this?" I asked, pulling the phone from my ear and not recognizing the number.

"This is Danielle. I was calling to see if you had any more tickets. I've sold half of mine already."

My eyes drifted to the clock on my car radio. I hadn't been away from her for two hours and she'd already sold twenty-five tickets? She had to be lying.

"Sure. I've got some more. Where do you want to meet to give me the money for the ones you sold and pick up some more?"

"Well, I wanna try to get off of the rest of them first, but can you come by my crib around seven this evening? I should be home by then."

"Yeah, text me your address and I'll meet you there," I said, before hanging up the phone.

Normally, I didn't go to my girls' houses. That was a line I tried to keep clear. But I didn't have shit else to do with Nel being on some bullshit, so I figured why not. And it would give me the chance to get to know her better. Especially if she could get off of fifty tickets in less than twenty-four hours.

My phone rang again. This time it was Nel. I let it go to voicemail. I hated to leave her sick and without anyone to take care of her, but she wasn't gonna treat me like a fuck nigga and think I was gonna let that shit slide. This would be her first and last time, whether because she learned her lesson or because I left her ass alone. I picked up my phone to let Shawn know what's up.

"Yo, Shawn... whattup bruh?... Yeah, just tryna make it man... Look, Sheila got in her feelings today and I had to leave her to make some decisions... yeah, man, you know how women are. But, do me a favor and go check on her for me? 'Precite it... Aight. Later."

I felt better knowing that Shawn would look in on Nel. I knew she had her family, but they had lives of their own, if her stubborn ass called them at all. I would give her a day and hit her up tomorrow to see if she'd found her mind.

Pulling into Summerchase Apartments, I went to check my mail first. I spent so much time at Nel's house that I only made it to the crib once or twice a week. Most of what I got was ads anyway. I walked up the walkway and up the stairs to the house. When I opened the door, I breathed in the scents of the Egyptian Gold oil that was sitting in my burner. I lit the tea candle, went into my fridge and grabbed a Heineken, and sat down in my La-Z-Boy. I turned on the TV but wasn't really watching it. My thoughts drifted to Nel. Sheila Price had had my attention before I even walked into her office. I had a great deal of respect for her business mind and her reputation. Maybe I should've stayed behind that glass.

Don't get me wrong, she's a great woman. Loving. Supportive. An awesome mother. But she had some real issues. She was so used to dealing with fuck niggas that she didn't know how to let somebody love her. But I was getting tired. I drank my beer and got lost in my thoughts. She only had one time to come with the bullshit and she'd spent it today.

*****

At six thirty, I got in my car to head to Danielle's. My GPS said she lived in Peppertree Apartments. I turned on 97.9 Jamz at full blast and made my way there. I needed to drown out my thoughts. Nel had me trippin'. I needed to go to Danielle's with a clear head so I could feel her out.

I knocked on the door and a thick red-headed white chick opened it. I thought I was in the wrong place until she smiled and told me that Danielle was in the back and was waiting for me. I walked into the house and had a seat on the couch. Looking around, the place was laid. I wondered if it was the white girl or Danielle paying the bills.

"So, you're Mr. Blowemup, huh?" the girl asked, sitting in the arm chair across from me.

"That's me," I said, smiling.

"I'm Bridgette, Danielle's girlfriend. I've heard all about you!"

"Oh yeah? Good things, I hope," I said, realizing I was flirting.

I thought it was sexy as hell that two bad ass women like Danielle and Bridgette fucked each other every night. I had to control my erection because the image alone had my dick jumping.

"All good things," she said, leaning in and so I could see her breasts through the V-neck of her shirt. "You want something to eat? I cooked chili. Or a beer or something?"

She was definitely the homemaker. I smiled even harder at the fact that Danielle was probably the one taking charge of her ass in the bedroom.

"Yeah, I'll take a beer. You gotta a Heineken?" I asked, not sure if I wanted to take my chances with her cooking.

"Coming right up," she said, getting up from her seat. "Is a chilled mug ok?"

"Yeah," I said, paying more attention to her ass than what she was asking. Snow bunny's ass was fat.

Ahem. Danielle cleared her throat as she entered the room, a broad smile across her face because she'd caught me staring at her girl's ass.

"Hey there, Ron. How are you?"

"I'm good," I said, trying not to show my embarrassment at getting caught.

"It's alright. That fat ass is one of the reasons I'm with her. Her cooking is another reason," she said to me before turning her attention towards the kitchen. "Hey Baby, bring me some of that chili and a Corona. And bring Ron some chili, too."

I sat and watched her body language soften when she turned back to me. She was wearing a Victoria's Secret Pink sweat suit with the jacket unzipped far enough for it to be seen that she didn't have a bra on. I'd peeped that she was missing a panty line, too, when she walked over to sit in the arm chair that Bridgette had been in before her. I knew I needed to get my ass outta here before I started thinking with the wrong head, but I was curious. I figured it would be rude not to eat the chili and drink the beer that was being prepared for me. But then I would get the money, give her the tickets, and take my ass back to Prattville.

Bridgette sat a steaming bowl of chili and my beer in a chilled glass on the table in front of me. Then she took Danielle hers and sat in her lap, both of them watching me. I scooped a spoonful of chili and blew it before I put it in my mouth. I had to admit, the shit was good. I sat back, my bowl in my lap, and enjoyed the meal while watching Bridgette feed Danielle her chili. That shit was almost erotic.

All of my common sense told me to get the fuck outta there, so I guzzled down my beer and stood, pulling another fifty tickets out of my pocket. I marked down the numbers in my tablet and handed them to Danielle. Bridgette got up and sauntered to the back to get the money. It took everything in me not to watch her ass walk down the hallway.

"You tryna leave so soon?" Danielle asked, stifling a giggle at my obvious struggle with my manhood.

"Yeah, I gotta get outta here. Got business to handle early in the morning," I said, telling a half-truth. The only business I had to handle was Nel.

"You sure? You don't look too good. You took that beer pretty quickly. Maybe you should have a seat and wait for Beth to get back with the money."

Beth? Who the hell is Beth? I thought her name was Bridgette, I thought to myself.

I was feeling kinda lightheaded and figured it was because this was my fourth beer of the night. I'd downed three before I got here thinking about the shit with Nel.

"Yeah, I'll sit down. But I gotta go," I emphasized, letting her know I was serious.

I sat down on the couch and felt my eyes getting heavy. I was in no condition to drive. I was gonna rest my eyes a little bit and then head out when I knew I was alright to get myself home, or at least to Nel's house in one piece.

"Hey, Danielle, you got any coffee in there?" I asked, noticing that my speech was slurred.

Something wasn't right. I wanted to move but I couldn't.

"Delilah, what you wanna do with him?" I heard Bridgette, or Beth, say.

Then, darkness.

Anthony

I walked into the living room as Delilah and Beth were standing over Ron's unconscious body. They were waiting on me so that I could record them having sex with him to send to Sheila. I wasn't really feeling the shit, but I wanted Sam's money so I had to deal with these two triflin' bitches until I got it. Setting up the tripod. They wasted no time getting started. They pulled down his jogging pants and Delilah sucked his dick until it stood at attention.

He moved, making them pause to make sure that he wasn't going to completely come-to. He mumbled a little but didn't snap out of it. They'd put enough damn tranquilizers in his food and beer to knock out a bear, so I wasn't worried. My part in the plan was to record them fuckin' him, help get his ass into his car, back home, and into his house so that he wouldn't remember what happened.

Delilah straddled his dick as soon as she saw the red record light come on. She rode him like her life depended on it while Beth kissed him, sucking on his neck, leaving hickeys all over it. He responded, lifting his hands groggily to hold onto Delilah's hips. He started moaning Nel's name, making Beth force her tongue into his mouth so that there was no record of him being out of it. He opened his eyes and seemed to realize what was going on.

Delilah took Beth's breast into her mouth and, surprisingly, he didn't try to protest. But what man would? Even if he realized he'd been drugged, he had two beautiful women fucking him and each other in front of him. Some men would die for this opportunity.

I smirked. I knew this nigga didn't love Sheila. He's just latching onto her so that he can expand his career here in Montgomery. I couldn't *wait* until she got this video. I didn't know what Delilah and Beth had planned, and I didn't care. But I knew, as soon as she got it, she would come running back to me. And that's all I cared about.

I looked up and Beth was on top of Ron now. She was so sexy, her soft ass jiggling in his lap. As a thank you, Delilah made her way over to me and dropped to the floor, pulling my dick out and wrapping her warm mouth around it. My knees buckled and I found my way back into the arm chair. She deep throated my dick, looking up into my eyes. That shit was spellbinding. I squirted down her throat and she stood up with a smirk.

Grabbing a handful of her braids, I turned her ass around and bent her over the chair. I massaged my dick with my free hand until I was hard and shoved myself into her. I drilled her ass like there was no tomorrow. I was pissed off that I was stuck with her ass, pissed about Sheila fuckin' with this sloppy ass nigga, and most of all, pissed that I was stuck with Sam's ass until this shit played out.

I came, hard, and when I let Delilah up, she pushed me back in the chair and go on top of me, riding me backwards. She and Beth watched each other as they fucked themselves into orgasm, using Ron and me as living dildos. I thought the shit was sexy as hell until I felt Delilah stop and stare at Beth, her head turning to the side. Beth must have been enjoying Ron too much for Delilah's liking. I started fuckin' Delilah from up under her. I didn't give a fuck about their lover's quarrel, I wanted to get my nut. When I did, I pushed Delilah off of me and got up to wash up.

When I came out of the bathroom, they were putting their clothes back on.

"Get this nigga outta my house," Delilah said staring at Beth.

I couldn't help but laugh a little at the way these two chickens were at each other's throats.

"Baby, chill. I had to make it look good for the camera," Beth pleaded.

"What the fuck ever. You were enjoying that shit. I know the face you make when some shit is good to you," Delilah said, looking like she was ready to slap the shit out of Beth.

"Look man, I got an idea," I said, standing in between them.

Delilah's head snapped in my direction.

"What?" she yelled, not hiding her anger.

"Let's drop his ass off outside of Sheila's house. Beth got hickeys all over him. He's got your lipstick on his dick and he smells like both of y'all. If we take him home, he'll have the chance to clean up and shit," I said proud of my quick thinking.

"Hell yeah," Delilah said, smiling at me. "And I'll call that bitch to let her know he's out there."

Delilah and I lifted Ron up off the couch and carried him to his car. I put him in the passenger's seat and headed down Vaughn Road to Sheila's house. Delilah followed me in Beth's car, parking a block away so that no one saw it. I parked the car, got out, and walked back to Delilah with a broad smile on my face.

I'm not a lowdown dude, but I had to do what I had to do. My brother-in-law, Matt, had bought the rest of the towing business from me after getting arrested for rape. He said it was bad for business for me to be working in an occupation that had a clientele base of over ninety percent females. I had to agree. I had gotten enough side eyes to last me a lifetime. It's amazing how fast bad news traveled in this little ass city. I was even taking a background position with the Mojo Lounge at Samantha's request. Shit was frustrating.

We got back to their apartment and Beth was gone. I could see the frustration in Delilah's face as she checked for messages and tried to call her with no answer. I didn't trust Beth. But Delilah was whipped and she wasn't thinking straight. As long as I got my dick wet from one of them, or both, and my plan went through, I could give a fuck less. I walked up on Delilah and kissed her on the nape of her neck. I knew that would get her excited. I wasn't ready to go home to Sam just yet and I knew that she was feeling low so she would be down for a good fuck.

She turned around with tears in her eyes. I don't think I'd ever seen her cry before. I looked at her and she broke down in front of me. I wrapped my arms around her and let her get it all out. Walking her to the couch, she laid her head on my shoulder, and cried until she was shaking.

"Delilah, what's wrong?" I finally asked.

"She's with Sam. I know it," she said, crying again.

"Yeah, you're probably right," I agreed.

"Why can't I find somebody to love me? Sam has you. Sheila has you. Sheila has Ron. Tammy and Tyrone got married. Scooter is even planning to go to Florida with the money we're paying him to try and get his baby mama back. Nobody wants me," she sobbed.

"Maybe you should take your money and leave Alabama. I mean, we're about to get Sam for all she's got, so why not forget about the whole revenge thing with Sheila and just move on. I'm sure you'll find somebody. You might just need a change of scenery," I suggested.

Smack!

Before I knew it, Delilah had slapped the shit outta me.

"What the fuck is wrong with you?" I yelled pushing her off me and getting up, ready to hit her ass back.

"See! You could've told me you love me but instead you're trying to get rid of me! Everybody is always trying to get rid of me! I'm good enough to fuck but not good enough to keep," she yelled, her eyes wide. She looked dangerous. I knew it was time to leave. I wasn't gonna be the one she took her anger out on.

I started backing towards the door. I wasn't nobody's punk, but that bitch was unstable and you never turn your back on an unstable woman. I twisted the lock and then the knob, keeping my eyes on Delilah. When I opened the door, I slid out of it and started jogging to my car. Hell, I was better off with Sam than this crazy bitch. Beth was gonna have hell to pay when she got home, though. *Not my problem*, I laughed to myself. Getting in my car and pulling off headed towards the house.

Beth

I pulled up into the parking lot of the Residence Inn Hotel. Tre called and said he had some information that I might find valuable. I was curious and, even though I knew that Delilah would be pissed because I wasn't there when she and Anthony got back from dropping Ron at Sheila's house, I was willing to take the chance. I was tired of her whopping my ass because of her inadequacy issues. I was gonna do something that I wanted to do.

I looked at my phone and saw it was Delilah calling. I put my phone back in my purse and checked to make sure my gun was in there, too. I didn't trust Tre or Scooter. They weren't the kind of people I'd fuck with, but Delilah swore that they were cool, so I took her word for it.

I walked up to room 115 and knocked. Tre opened the door, wearing nothing but a wife beater and a pair of boxer briefs. Against my better judgment, I walked in.

"So, what's up?" I asked wanting to get this shit over with.

"Sit down, Snow Bunny. Ain't nobody gonna hurt you."

I walked over to the chair and sat down, keeping my purse in my lap. I hated when people call me Snow Bunny like I didn't know I was a white girl. That shit wasn't cute. I looked around the room, Scooter was nowhere to be found. That made me kinda uneasy.

"Look, you said you had something to tell me that you didn't want to tell me over the phone or while I was around Delilah. What is it?"

He laughed. Looking me up and down before licking his full lips. I felt my skin begin to crawl. I was starting to think that I had made a mistake coming here.

"How well do you know Delilah?" he asked, sitting on the bed, an obvious erection showing through his boxer briefs.

"I only met her about six months ago. We hit it off immediately. Why?" I wanted him to get to the point so I could go see Samantha before I went back home to deal with Delilah's bullshit.

"So you don't know anything about her past?" he asked with his eyebrow raised.

"Past? What past? I mean, I know Samantha is her half-sister. They have the same daddy," I shared what I knew. "I know she's from Tuskegee."

"Look Snow Bunny, you seem like a nice girl and I don't want you to get sucked into Delilah's bullshit. Bad shit happens to everyone who comes into contact with that psycho bitch. She held my dick at gunpoint when we were dating. Accused me of fuckin' her momma. Her daddy used to fuck her. He got locked up when Delilah called the cops on his ass for doin' that shit. And her momma... well, she killed her momma. They got into it about her daddy and about me and she burned the house down. *With her momma in it.* Spent four years in the psych ward behind that shit."

I couldn't believe what I was hearing. Delilah had had a fucked up life. No wonder she was so high strung. I felt a pain in my heart for her. But I had to wonder why Tre was sharing this information with me.

"That bitch you sleep beside every night is a coldblooded killer. I want you to be careful. When you don't serve a purpose for her anymore, she might just kill you, too."

"And why should I listen to anything you have to say? You choked your girl with a belt and shot her."

His jaw tightened. I could tell I'd hit a nerve.

"Listen, I don't know yo' ass from any other dyke bitch who gotta sweet tooth for chocolate. I ain't gone get nothing outta tellin' you this. Hell, I might be fuckin' myself outta whole lot of money. I know you loyal to Dee, but I don't wanna see you hurt. You seem like good people. But you can take what you want from what I said," he said, shrugging his shoulders.

The bed squeaked when he got up. He walked over to the nightstand. Opening the drawer, he pulled out a sack and a Cigarillo. He sat back down before breaking down the cigar and dumping the insides into the trash can. He filled the cigar with weed. I sat there stuck in my thoughts. After what he'd just told me, I worried about my life fuckin' with Delilah. I didn't know how I'd gotten caught up with her and her nonsense. There was only so much that my dad could get me out of. And I'd never needed his help until I met Delilah.

Tre finished rolling his blunt and sparked it up. I watched him pull on it, hold it in, and then blow the smoke out of his nose slowly. I heard the door open and Scooter walked in with some Popeye's. He looked at Tre, then at me, and smiled.

"Awww shit! What's up, Snow Bunny?" he greeted me.

"Hey Scooter," I answered, about tired of that damn nickname.

"Am I interrupting something?" he asked, beaming at Tre.

"No, I was just leaving," I said, getting up from the chair and walking to the door.

"Yo, watch that bitch. For real, Beth," Tre said, a look of seriousness on his face.

I walked out of the hotel room and to my Hyundai Sonata. I didn't know what Tre's motive was, but I knew I'd better heed his warning. My life may depend on it.

Samantha

The alarm chimed and I heard footsteps headed towards our spare bedroom. Kris and I hadn't slept in the same bed since he got out of jail. The sight of him nauseated me. I'd fully recovered from the abortion and hadn't talked to Tyrone since the day I went upside his head. I figured he would've at least checked to see if I was ok, but I guess he was too busy playing husband to that hoe Tammy. The thought of it pissed me off, but who was I to say anything. I was married when I got with him, wasn't supposed to get pregnant, and then had an abortion when he chose Tammy over me.

I was playing a dangerous game with a man who didn't play games. But I thought he loved me. I mean *really* loved me. But just like Kris, he fucked around on me. At least Kris hadn't left me for anyone else. Even with all of his fuckin' around, he was still here. I needed to appreciate that.

I checked my phone again, seeing if there was anything from Beth. There wasn't.

"Fuck it," I said, getting up and washing up.

I put on a purple lace teddy and some black patent leather pumps and made my way to the spare bedroom. The door was closed. I could hear moans coming from the other side of the door. I immediately became angry because I knew he'd snuck some bitch into our house. I knocked and heard shuffling and the moaning stop abruptly. I knocked again.

Kris came to the door wearing nothing. I could tell that he wasn't pleased with the interruption.

"Can I help you?" he asked, a scowl stuck on his face.

"You got company?" I asked, knowing that it would piss him off.

"It's my house, too, Samantha. What if I do? Are you watchin' what I do again? Is there a nanny cam in this fuckin' room, too?"

"No," I stumbled, realizing he was still mad about a lot of shit. "I was just hopin' we could ummm..." I stumbled.

"What? You want to fuck? Your bitch must not be answering the phone."

I realized that I'd made a mistake. I should have stayed my ass in my room. I don't know what the hell I was thinking.

"Never mind, Kris," I said, turning to walk away.

"You're never gonna apologize to me for the shit you did to me, huh?" he yelled at my back.

"Apologize to *you*? You fucked around on me with Sheila, Delilah, *and* Beth? And there were probably other random bitches I haven't found out about yet. But you think I should apologize to *you*? You had how many outside babies on me? You leave me in the house with these children or leave them for your mother or sister to keep while you're out doin' *God knows what* but you have the nerve to say I should be apologizing to you. You have got to be the outside your motherfuckin'..."

Before I could finish my rant, he grabbed me and kissed me. He had a handful of my ass and I melted like butter. I needed to be touched. At this point, it didn't matter by who. But Kris's touch could always make me weak in the knees. We kissed, our tongues wrestling for control, for so long I started to leak down my thigh. Kris broke our kiss and looked deep into my eyes. No words needed to be spoken. He turned me around, pressing me up against the wall, palms up like I was being frisked. He used his feet to kick my legs open and, while holding my hands together with one hand, he guided his dick into me with the other.

"Ahhhh, Kris," I moaned, my voice echoing off the wall.

"Shut up," he ordered, giving me every inch of himself.

I obeyed. Pressing my face against the wall and taking the pained pleasure that he was giving me. I felt his heartbeat as his chest pressed up against my back. Trying to remain quiet made me wetter. I was cumming all over his dick. He let out a grunt, letting me know he was about to cum and I felt him jerk, his weight pressing me against the wall.

I opened my eyes to see a light-skinned woman with a bob cut standing, naked in the doorway of the spare bedroom. I felt stupid all over again. He'd jumped straight from her pussy to mine. This man had no morals and no concern for my health.

"What the fuck!" I yelled, pushing off of the wall, making him stumble backwards.

He looked at the woman in the doorway and then at me. There was no remorse in his eyes at all.

"Really, Anthony?" the woman yelled, storming back into the room, I assumed to get dressed.

"Keisha!" he yelled, running back to the room and closing the door, leaving me there to nurse my own aching heart.

I heard screaming and then nothing. I stood there, waiting for her to storm out of the room and out of my fuckin' house. But then, the moans started again. I couldn't take it anymore. I walked back to my room, feeling defeated. Even when I fucked Beth in the house, I made sure Kris wasn't there, or he was asleep. I laid in my bed and cried. I thought about Tyrone and how he used to hold me and make me feel secure. How he used to look at me like I was the only woman in the world and when we were together, no one else mattered.

I ached for him. Even though I knew he was married, I needed to talk to him. I picked up my phone to call him.

"The number you have dialed has been disconnected or is no longer in service," the operator informed me.

I had never felt so alone in my life.

Delilah

"I know this bitch see me callin' her. When she gets here I'm gone whoop her motherfuckin' ass," I said to myself, pacing the bedroom.

Beth had lost her mind thinking that she was gonna leave here without me knowin' where she was goin' and not answer when I called her. I was so mad I could spit fuckin' fire! That bitch must not know who the fuck she was dealin' with. I heard the door open, mid-pace, and made my way to the front of the apartment.

"Where the hell you been?" I asked, before she was in the house good.

"I went..."

I slapped the shit out of her before she could get the lie out of her mouth.

"Don't fuckin' lie to me!" I screamed.

She slapped me back, shocking the hell out of me because she'd never fought me back before. Whoever she'd been fuckin' had given her some confidence. I needed to remedy that shit immediately.

I reached back and jabbed her right in the mouth. When she stumbled backwards, I took advantage and hit her with a hook and another jab before grabbing her hair and dragging her down the hallway. Beth kicked and screamed with everything that she had in her, but that didn't stop me. When we made it into the bedroom, I flung her on the floor, kicking her in her stomach.

She balled up into the fetal position while I wailed on her and kicked her until I was tired. Whatever nigga or bitch she was with wasn't gonna want her ass anymore. I sat on the edge of the bed trying to catch my breath. I looked down at Beth who was on the floor whimpering, and thought about starting in on her ass again. I stood up and my phone rang. Walking past her, I went to the living room to get my phone off the table.

"Hello," I answered, still out of breath.

"Hey there, Sweetness," a man said.

The hair stood on the back of my neck. Only one person called me that. But I knew that it couldn't be him. I pulled my phone away from my ear and looked at the caller ID. The number was showing up private.

"Wh-who is this?" I asked, praying for it to be anyone else.

"You know who this is," he snickered.

"What do you want?" I tried to sound brave.

"I want you," he said, making me get sick to my stomach. "Now, are you gonna come to me or are you gonna make me come find you?"

"Fuck you. You're not gonna find me. So, take your ass on some damn where," I said hanging up the phone.

I immediately called Tre's phone.

"What's up, Dee," he asked, sounding nervous.

"Look man, I want you to stop all tracking of Tammy and Tyrone. I gotta more pressing issue that I need you to handle for me."

"Ok, what you need?" he asked me.

"Look man, I can't discuss this shit over the phone. Can I come to the room?"

"Yeah. Come on," he said, sounding annoyed.

That nigga better be grateful that his ass wasn't rotting in a cell. If it wasn't for me, him and Scooter would be in jail being bent over somewhere. I went back into the room and put on my shoes. I grabbed my keys and purse and walked over Beth, who was still on the floor, kicking her one last time.

She better clean up that mess she made on my damn floor before I get back here, I know that, I thought to myself.

I got in my car headed to the Residence Inn.

*****

When I got to the hotel, I knocked on the door to room 115. Scooter answered the door.

"What's up, Dee?" he asked as I pushed my way into the room. "Ain't no reason to be rude, man. What the fuck is your problem?"

"Look, man, I ain't got no time to waste," I said frowning up at the smell of weed that hung in the air.

"What you want Delilah?" Tre asked me, rolling a blunt the size of his thumb.

"I just got an interesting call," I sat down in the chair.

"Ok. What does that have to do with me?" he asked, licking the cigar.

"Nothing at all," I said frustrated.

Tre lit the blunt. He pulled on it and blew the smoke into the room. He never looked at me. It was pissing me off that he was treating me like I was irrelevant.

"Dee, come on, man. Don't come up in here killing the vibe," Scooter said walking over and taking the blunt from Tre.

"Bitch don't kill my vibe. Bitch don't kill my vibe," Tre's high ass sang, co-signing Scooter's request.

"Man, fuck y'all," I said getting up and walking over to take the blunt from Scooter. "Samson Powell called me tonight."

They both stopped laughing. I puffed on the blunt and choked, holding the smoke in.

"Who?" they said in unison, both seeming to sober just a little.

"You heard me," I said finally blowing the smoke out through my nose.

"Oh shit," Scooter sat down.

I kept smoking the blunt because neither of them seemed interested anymore. They owed Samson thousands of dollars. When he got locked up, they took over Tuskegee and, after a while, they stopped putting money on his books. They left him in there to rot. Now he was out and we needed to figure out how to take his ass out.

Samson was my, and Samantha's, daddy. He molested me for as long as I can remember and when I started my period, he started fuckin' me. I finally called the cops when I met Tre. The plan was to get Samson out of the picture so Tre and Scooter could take over and I was gonna be the Empress to the Empire. But then I found out Tre was fuckin' my momma so I had to get her ass out of the picture, too.

Once I thought I had eliminated every threat, along came Tammy's ass. So, to stay close to Tre, I started fuckin' with his flunky, Scooter. I never expected to fall for his triflin' ass, though. I befriended Tammy and, one night when we were having a sleepover, I turned her ass out. I planned to work my way back into Tre's good graces, but, instead of him choosing me over Tammy, he and Scooter started tag teaming our asses. But Tre made it clear that Tammy was his main and Scooter went and got that bitch Cheyenne pregnant. And now here we were.

"Look man, that nigga gone kill us if he find us," Tre said, obviously shaken by the news.

"That's why we've gotta find him first," I said passing him the blunt.

We started scheming on how to get Samson out of the picture for good.

Tanisha

"Hey Tanni."

I heard a voice that made me stop dead in my tracks. I was scared to death to turn around because I knew what him being back in my life would mean. I stood frozen at the door to my apartment.

"You gonna just stand there?" he asked, a smile in his voice. He lived on the fear that he instilled in others.

I turned around to face him. He looked damn good. But even the devil came cloaked in shiny robes when he approached Eve in the Garden of Eden. He smiled at me, the smile that had taken me to hell and back. The smile that had me considering buying a ticket to hell again.

Towering over me at six-foot-five inches, his chocolate skin was smooth as silk. His beard and mustache were littered with gray hair, but that was sexy as hell to me. He was dressed in a wife beater and some gray sweatpants. If you looked at him, you wouldn't know he was a lying manipulative bastard who would cut your throat without blinking.

"Hello, Samson," I said trying to disguise my fear behind a smile. But I knew he could see through the shit. He always could.

"I'm not gonna bite you, Tanni. Unless you want me to," he said licking his full lips. The lips my child inherited. Those lips could talk a nun out of her panties.

"What can I do for you, Samson?" I asked with my keys in my hand.

"You can let me in," he said in a tone that was more a command than a request.

I turned and opened the door, doing as I was told. As soon as we were in my apartment, he grabbed a handful of my ass.

"Samson, I've got AIDS," I said hoping that would deter him.

"So do I," he smiled at me. "So we might as well fuck each other."

I turned my head to the side, completely thrown off by what he'd just told me. I wanted to ask questions, but it'd been so long since I'd been touched that I was just happy someone was willing to. Samson wasted no time pulling his dick out of his pants and, as if it were thirty years ago, I instinctively dropped to my knees and took him into my mouth. He held the back of my head and guided himself in and out of my mouth.

I had a flashback.

Samson was my pimp. I met him one night when I was out turning a few tricks to get money for me and Tyrone some food after his daddy abandoned us. Samson took one look at me and told me I was too beautiful to be fuckin' for chump change. He moved me and Tyrone out the projects and into one of his rental houses in Montgomery. I thought he was in Real Estate. It turned out that was how he cleaned his money. He was the Dope King in Tuskegee and Auburn. He started slangin' crack when it first made its appearance in the eighties.

We had a great life. Samson was good to us and made sure I stayed flyy. He paid me to count his money and all shipments came to our house. He loved Tyrone because he said he'd always wanted a son. And then I found out he was married. AND had a mistress in Tuskegee. I wasn't gonna be number three to anyone. When I went off on him, he kicked my ass and told me I belonged to him and as long as he wanted me to. Then he told me that since I wanted to cause a problem, I was gonna have to earn my keep.

He started trickin' me out to his supplier and anyone else who came to him talking big money. I started sneaking and snorting coke to deal with the shit he was putting me through. Then I came up pregnant with Sheila. The reason she had the heart issues that she had was because I didn't stop using, even while I was pregnant. When Sheila was born, the nurse told Samson she had cocaine in her system. I came home to mine and Tyrone's shit being thrown out in the street. I went back to the projects, now trickin' to satisfy my addiction. Samson came back around after I got my ass beat and robbed, saying that I needed his protection. He started pimpin' me, but I was willing to do anything to keep him in my life. Even sold Tyrone to some of the tricks because they preferred little boys. And on those lonely nights, especially after Samson got locked up, I started having sex with my son.

I was brought back from my painful and embarrassing past by Samson slapping me in the face with his dick before cumming all over my face.

"Get up," he ordered. "Go wash your face and come here so I can get that pussy and that ass."

I rose to my feet. I went to the bathroom and washing his sperm off of my face. I walked back into the living room to find him on the couch naked. Prison had done him good. His body was chiseled into a masterpiece. I found myself salivating at the sight of it. Walking over to the couch, I watched him massage himself into another erection. I got ready to straddle him when he got up.

"Bend over," he commanded.

I bent over the arm of the couch and he squatted and shoved his dick inside of me. I hollered and he put his hand over my mouth to shut me up while he rammed his dick into me violently. He fucked me fast and hard. Even though it hurt, I kept cumming over and over again. He bent down and bit into my shoulder. He grabbed me around my throat and made me stand upright while he rammed his pelvis into my ass. He pulled out, bending down and spreading my ass cheeks. He stuck his tongue into my ass and, when I came from that, he spit on my asshole before easing his dick in.

I wanted to scream but I knew better. I bit my bottom lip as tears streamed down my face. He was way too big to be in anyone's ass but I stood there, body leaned back over the couch as he ripped my asshole open. He picked up the pace and I knew he was about to cum.

"Delilah. Ughhhh Delilah," he grunted, cumming in my ass.

He used to call me that when we were dating. I was just happy that he remembered. That made me feel special. I was his Delilah and he was my Samson. We both had been given a death sentence but until the Grim Reaper came, we were gonna be together.

Sheila

I walked outside to take the trash out and saw Ron's car in the driveway. I felt my heart jump because I knew I'd fucked up and pushed him away by acting insecure. I flung the trash into the can and walked over to the driver's side. Knocking on the window, I tried to wake him up. He stirred a little bit and I saw that his pants were unzipped and his dick was out. I felt anger begin to stir inside of me and knocked on the window a little bit harder. He opened his eyes and looked at me but I could tell that he'd been drinking or something because he wasn't registering who I was. He turned his head away from me and I spotted a big ass hickey on his neck.

Now, mad as hell. I started beating on the window even harder, not caring if I broke it. He had some nerve going out and getting drunk then fuckin some bitch and bringin' his ass to my house like I was gonna be ok with it. He wasn't responding to my beating and my anger turned to worry. What if he'd had too much to drink and had alcohol poisoning? What if he drank to drown out the dumb shit I'd said to him? I needed to get him some help.

I reached into my pocket and started 911 but changed my mind when I realized that the cops would lock his ass up for driving under the influence. I called Tyrone instead.

"Hello?" he answered, sleep still in his voice.

"Hey Ty, I need your help," I said, trying to sound calm.

"What's up, Nel? You ok?"

"Yeah. I'm fine. But Ron's not. We got into a fight and he left yesterday afternoon. I came out this morning to take out my trash and he's passed out in his car."

"Did you call 911?" he asked the next logical question.

"No, because they're gonna lock him up for DUI if they come and find him like this. I need to get him in the house."

"Well, if he's stupid enough to drive under the influence, they should lock his ass up," Ty said, still being reasonable.

"Ty, look. Ron can drink like a fish. For him to be this far gone, something is seriously wrong. His pants are open and he's got hickeys and shit on his neck. I think somebody might have drugged him."

"Or he got drunk and fucked around on you," Ty countered my assumption.

"Look, he's not that kinda dude, ok. Just come help me, *please*," I begged.

"Fine, Nel. I'll be there in a few. I hope you right about him," Ty cautioned, his voice telling me that if I was wrong, Ron had an ass whoopin' comin'.

"Thank you, Ty," I hung up.

I was weak from my radiation so I became lightheaded. Knocking hadn't worked so I figured I would just wait for Ty to get here. I slowly walked back to the house. I became nauseated and puked into my garden. I eased back into the house and into my room, collapsing on the bed. I came to when I heard Tammy's voice in my ear.

"Nel... Nel... wake up," she said, putting her hand on my forehead. "Damn baby, she's got a fever," she said, I assumed to Tyrone.

I opened my eyes to see both their worried faces standing over me. I tried to smile, but that took too much effort. I cleared my throat and tried to speak.

"Whe-where's Ron," I asked, concerned.

"I put him on the couch. He's barely conscious but he said the new model he'd hired did this to him. Said she told him her name was Danielle but he heard her girlfriend call her Delilah before he passed out," Ty explained, anger in his voice.

"Did you tell him about Delilah, Nel?" Tammy asked.

I shook my head no.

"Then that bitch is out and causin' drama," Ty said, his face turning red. "Ain't nobody got time for her or her shit."

I frowned, my mind racing because I didn't know that Delilah was out or how she knew about me and Ron. I wanted to get angry but I was too weak. I tried to sit up but Tammy placed her hand on my shoulder.

"No ma'am," she said, emphatically. "You're gonna lay down and rest. Ron will be just fine. You can't afford to get all worked up. We'll take care of Delilah," she said looking at Tyrone then back at me.

I laid back down and closed my eyes. Before I knew it I'd drifted back to sleep.

*****

I woke up to Ron sitting on the side of my bed. He looked really worried. As badly as I wanted to be mad at him, I knew that he wasn't the cheating type and I wanted to hear him out.

"Hey baby," he smiled at me.

"You ok?" I asked, easing up in the bed.

"Yeah. I got the hangover from hell, but I'm ok," he said, trying to joke.

"Ain't shit funny," I said, angrily. "How the hell did you end up drunk, passed out in my driveway, with your dick out and hickeys on your neck?" I asked, my voice weak.

"I don't know how I got here, Nel. All I remember was going to my model Danielle's house to get the money for the tickets she'd sold and to give her some more tickets. Her and her girlfriend offered me something to eat and something to drink. I don't remember anything else after that and I woke up here," he explained.

"Danielle? I thought you told Ty you heard somebody call her Delilah," I questioned, not feeling so well.

"I did," he admitted. "Before I passed out."

"And this girlfriend was a white girl with red hair and freckles and a big ass?"

"Yeah. What the fuck is going on, baby?" Ron asked, looking like he was ready to kill somebody.

I cleared my throat and filled Ron in on the last few months' events. Things I never thought I would have had to tell him about.

Anthony

I laid in bed, my arms wrapped around Keisha. Her fat ass wiggled against my dick making it stand at attention. I knew I was playing a dangerous game bringing her in the house while Sam was here. The last time I did that shit, it didn't end well for me. But at this point, I didn't care. Until Sam divorced me, this was my house, too. And I'd tried to fix things with her when I got out of jail but she wasn't hearing it. So, fuck her. She made her bed, so she could go lay in it. *Alone.*

Keisha moved again. I cupped her C's in my hands, pinching on her nipples. She moaned, making my dick even harder. She reached back and spread her ass cheeks so I could slide in from the back. I pushed myself into her wetness and felt her tighten her muscles on my dick. She moaned over and over, loudly. She knew Sam was home and was trying to mark territory. That shit turned me on.

When she'd caught me fuckin' Sam, she was pissed, but she showed her crazy when, instead of getting dressed and leaving, she told me she was gonna show me her pussy was better. Before Sam's ass came knocking on the door, I'd been giving Keisha head while she watched porn on the big screen. But after she saw me fuck Sam, she was mad that she didn't get the dick first and, after sucking Sam's juices off of me, she rode my ass straight to sleep.

I laughed to myself as I fucked her. I had this terrible attraction to crazy. This woman couldn't be in her right mind to knowingly fuck another woman's husband in their house when the woman was there. But crazy always had the best pussy. I fucked Keisha hard. Ramming her ass and feeling the waves against my stomach as I drilled her.

We fucked like we didn't have a care in the world. And we didn't. I'd met her at a strip party Matt threw a couple of months ago. She was the main attraction but she'd let me put my fingers in her pussy at the party. Then pulled me into a room in the suite to give me a private dance and rode my face and let me fuck her before goin' home with her that night. We'd been rockin' ever since.

She'd asked me to move in with her after that shit went down with Samantha. Once I got this money from Sam, I was gonna take her up on that offer. I needed to get the hell away from here. I was tired of Samantha, Delilah, Beth, and knew I would never get Sheila back. My kids could come visit me so that wasn't enough to keep me here. And I had a feeling Samantha was gonna try to deny me my visitation in the divorce. But I was gonna fight for at least that. But that would happen once she filed for divorce.

"Ahhhh shit, Anthony! I'm about to cum," Keisha screamed.

Her body started convulsing and her muscles tightened around my dick. Then, wetness. I felt my dick tighten and she moved her ass in a circular motion, letting my dick hit all her walls. When I hit bottom, I squirted all inside of her and held her close as I started to doze off, my dick still in her.

My phone started to vibrate and I didn't even look to see who was calling. Whoever it was wasn't important enough to get me up outta Keisha. I felt her breathing get softer and knew she was out for the count. I started moving myself in and out of her until I was hard again. Sleep or not, I wasn't done. Her moving with me, even in her sleep, let me know that she wasn't done either.

I was gonna get it in before I had to walk out of the room to deal with Samantha's shit, walk out of the house and deal with Delilah and Beth's craziness, and go out into the world with a rape accusation taped to my back like a "kick me" sign.

Ron

Sheila had me pissed off all over again. I don't know why she didn't think she needed to tell me about all the shit that she went through right before we met, but that shit got me caught up. I ended up in a situation that could have gotten me killed. And I wouldn't have known why or what was going on. I sat there staring at her, trying not to go the hell off. She was really proving to be more of a problem than I wanted to deal with.

"Why the hell didn't you tell me any of this, Nel?" I asked, my teeth clenched.

"Because I thought the crazy bitch was gonna gone about her damn business," she said, sounding frightened.

"Well, apparently she's not done with you. And now, she's put me in the shit. I oughtta go and beat her ass," I said angrily, getting up from the bed.

"No, Ron, trust me. She's dangerous," Nel pled with me not to do anything stupid.

I sat back down but made a mental note to send somebody to go see about Delilah and her white bitch. I don't play like that. Tyrone came into the room.

"Yo, Ron, can I holla at you?" he asked with a serious look on his face.

"Yeah, man. I'll be back, Nel," I said, getting up and reluctantly kissing her on the forehead because I really wasn't feeling her like that right now.

We walked out of the bedroom and Ty led me out the door. He pulled out and lit a Newport before speaking. I joined him with my Black & Mild. He blew the smoke through his mouth and looked at me.

"Look, man. I know you mad as hell with Nel. Hell, I would be, too. She was trying to keep you around and was embarrassed about the shit that she's been through. That lets me know that she really cares about you. Normally, she doesn't give a damn about what people think about her."

"Yeah, I get that vibe from her," I laughed. "This is a lot of shit for a nigga to process, though. She could have told me somethin'. How am I supposed to protect her, or myself, if I don't know who the enemy is or what they're capable of?"

"Yeah, I feel you. Nel and Tammy are both bad about that shit. You just have to understand that they were both kinda left to fend for themselves, so letting a man be there for them is a foreign concept to them," he said, snickering.

"I got my work cut out for me, huh?" I asked him.

He just nodded. I had plenty to think about. I wanted to know the real about Delilah and Nel, though. The shit that I knew that she was holding back from me.

"So, tell me what's good, man. How unstable is this Delilah bitch?"

"Man, just watch her ass. She came in here and beat the hell out of Nel over the married man that they were both fuckin'. And Delilah *knew* that he was fuckin' Nel. But Nel didn't know about him and Delilah until she walked into Delilah's house and caught the nigga Anthony waist deep in her ass. Before that, she thought Delilah was her best friend. Hooked us all up for this lounge thang y'all are working on the grand opening for. Hell, Anthony's wife, my ex, hired her to do the promotions."

"The fuck?" I asked. My head was starting to hurt.

I swear if I didn't love Nel's ass, I would just get in my fuckin' car and go. What kinda fucked up luck did this woman have that all this shit happened to her. Maybe it was karma for her sleepin' with a married man.

"Man, the shit Nel has survived is unreal. So, I wanted to talk with you and let you know what was up because I know this shit is just getting started with Delilah. If she knows who you are, you're a target, too. I been lookin' over my shoulder for weeks now. And with Tammy pregnant, I'm really worried. That bitch is ruthless and I'd hate to have to put hands on her," he said, flicking the cigarette.

"I could handle her ass," I said, putting my black out against the brick wall.

Tyrone laughed. But he didn't tell me not to. The look on his face told me that he wished someone *would* get her ass out the picture. I decided right then to put my ears to the street. I would let my girls befriend Delilah and act like I didn't know what they did to me. And when she least expected it, I would get her. I wouldn't say anything to Nel or Tyrone. The less they knew, the better.

Tammy

I couldn't even enjoy my time celebrating our new baby with my husband before Nel called talking about something Delilah did to Ron. We got up and got dressed and went to her rescue *again*. I wondered if that would change when the baby got here or if Tyrone was gonna leave me in the house with our newborn while he came to Nel's rescue. Don't get me wrong, I love Nel. But she's too damn old to be expecting her brother to keep coming over to fix her messes.

If she'd told Ron about Delilah, shit wouldn't have happened the way that it did. Ron's a good man and didn't deserve to be left in the dark. Or dragged into the drama that came attached with being with anyone in this family. I wanted to warn him but it wasn't my place. I just waited for Tyrone to say we could go home, checking on Nel when he and Ron went out to talk.

"You ready baby?" Ty asked me as he and Ron made their way back into the house.

"You sure, Ty?" I asked, not wanting to have to turn back around and be here again in a matter of hours.

"Yeah, I think Nel and Ron can take it from here," he said, holding his hand out to me.

When I got up, he pulled me to him and kissed me on my forehead. I didn't want to seem too eager to go but I was. We walked towards the door and Ron headed to Sheila's bedroom. When we got in the car, I felt like I was about to explode.

"You gonna tell me what's up with you," Tyrone asked as he drove us home.

"Baby," I thought of what I wanted to say, "you gonna run to Nel's rescue like this when TJ gets here?"

He didn't say anything for a while. I knew he was thinking so I didn't say anything either. He pulled into the driveway and put the car in park. Neither of us moved to get out of it. He turned to me and reached for my hand. I didn't know if it was my hormones or not, but I felt tears streaming down my cheeks.

"You don't feel like a priority, huh? You knew the relationship I had with my sister before we got together. Why is it a problem now?" he asked, a frown on his face.

"Tyrone, I love Nel. I was the one holding her down when you were in jail. But, she's not a kid anymore. You've devoted your life and your time to making up for what you feel like you missed with your sister. But you have a wife and son now. It's time to let your sister be a grown-up."

He gritted his teeth. I could tell he didn't like what I was saying. But I wouldn't be being fair to myself if I wasn't honest with him about my feelings. I just didn't expect him to take it like this.

"Sheila needs me. She needed me and I wasn't there. I failed her. So, I won't neglect you and TJ, but I won't leave my sister to fend for herself, either."

"Tyrone, the reason you were away from her was because you jumped on Tre defending her. And that was behind a decision that she made. You lost *years* of your life because of her actions. You don't owe her anything. I need to know that you are gonna be here and able to make *your* family a priority."

Ty sighed and opened the door. He got out of the car and walked to the door. I sat there and cried. I cried for myself and the fact that I would always come second to his sister. I cried even harder for our son because at the rate Nel did shit, he may come into the world fatherless.

Tyrone

My baby sister has cancer and Tammy had the nerve to complain about me "coming to her rescue". I tried to hold in my frustration but I couldn't hide it. I was pissed. How *dare* Tammy ask me to choose between my son and my sister. They're both my family. And Sheila has cancer! Next, she was gonna ask me not to spend time with my mother, even though she was dying.

I walked into the house and poured myself a shot of Christian Brothers White Brandy. I needed a drink after the day I'd had. I took my drink into the spare room that served as my man cave. I didn't want to be bothered. I needed to think. I wanted to talk to someone. I picked up my phone to call someone but realized that the two people I always turned to, Tammy and Nel, were the ones causing me problems right now. I thought about who else I could talk to. I didn't know Ron well enough to call him and I sure as hell wasn't calling Anthony's bitch ass. I got upset at the realization that I'd devoted so much of my life to my sister, and now Tammy, that I had no one to turn to outside of them. Taking deep breaths, I fought back tears. I was lonely and frustrated.

"Fuck it," I said aloud to myself and dialed my sister's number.

"Hello?" she sounded like she was feeling a little bit better.

"Hey Nel."

"You alright, Ty?" she asked, sensing that something was wrong.

"No," I admitted. "Me and Tammy just got into a fight."

"What the hell about?" she asked like she was surprised that we'd fought.

"Well, you actually. She's pregnant and worried that I'm gonna put you ahead of her and our son," I explained.

"She's *pregnant*? When did you find out!" she screamed in my ear, ignoring the rest of what I'd said.

"She found out today. We were celebrating the news when you called me about Ron," I said, trying to refocus her on my problem.

"Well, you should have said something," she said it like I had a choice.

"Nel, you couldn't have gotten that man out of his car. You *needed* my help," I reminded her.

"Maybe I'll stop *needing* your help so much," she said, being a smart ass.

"What?" I asked, getting angry. If she didn't need the help, why the fuck was she always running to me. "What you mean?"

"Look, Ty, I know that you're married and now you've got a little miracle baby on the way. What kinda sister would I be if I didn't respect that? I think it's more a matter of you not wanting to let go. We've been through some real shit, but you've taken enough bullshit on my behalf. And I've got Ron now," she paused and I knew she was looking at him. "You need to let me clean up my own shit. I'm a grown-up and I need to be able to take care of myself."

I listened to her. I knew she was able to take care of herself but I felt like I'd failed her as a big brother growing up and wanted to fix that.

"You hear me, Tyrone?" she asked, breaking my train of thought. "You still feeling guilty and shit about our youth, about going to jail, about not being there for me. But you *were* there for me. You gave up years of your life because of my fuck up. You have a chance to have a life of your own. A *family* of your own. Why would I interfere with that? Now, get off the damn phone and go take care of your wife and my nephew. I'll be fine," she hung up before I could say anything.

I sat there and finished my drink. She was right, but I didn't want to hear that shit. I lit a Newport and then put it out realizing that I wasn't gonna be able to smoke in the house anymore. I didn't want to make Tammy sick and risk causing any issues with my son.

My son. The thought made me smile. I had another chance to be a father. A chance I never thought I was gonna have. I couldn't be happier. I needed to talk to my wife. I got up and walked out of my office and into our bedroom where Tammy was sitting with her head in her hands. She was sniffling and when she looked up at me, her nose was red. She was so cute. She deserved my undivided attention and, honestly, seeing her cry made me feel like a failure all over again. It was my job to love and protect her. Not to make her cry.

I mean, I knew I was gonna make her cry, especially now that she was pregnant. But I wanted it to be over some dumb shit I did from now on, not somebody else's drama.

"I think you should let someone buy you out of the Lounge," she said.

"Yeah, I think you're right. I don't like Anthony and Delilah's ass is still a partner and she's showin' that she's gonna be on some bullshit. I'll call Nel and tell her tomorrow. I'm pretty sure she'll understand."

"Really? You're willing to walk away from it? I was sure you were gonna put up a real fight about that one," she said, surprised.

"No need to fight with you about something that I know will cause nothing but stress for us, for *you*," I said. "I need you to be as stress-free as possible for little TJ," I said, smiling from ear-to-ear.

"TJ, huh?" she said, smiling and standing up. "Yep, Tyrone Jamaal Price," I said, not wanting to steal my son's identity by making him a Junior.

"I like that," she stood on her tiptoes and kissed me.

She stepped back and grinned at me before walking back over to the bed. I knew what that meant. I walked over to my side of the bed, taking my clothes off, never taking my eyes off of her. She was so beautiful. And she was mine. My wife. Pregnant with my son. I pulled her to me and she laid her head on my chest. I wanted to feel her but I needed to make sure she was ok first. I felt her breathing slow and I knew that she was asleep. I figured I'd join her. Then I heard glass break and gunshots. I jumped down on the floor, dragging Tammy with me. I laid on top of her, making sure not to put too much of my weight on her.

"Ty!" she screamed.

"Shhhhh," I silenced her. If somebody was shooting into our house, I wasn't gonna make us easy targets.

We laid there on the floor until there was a knock on the door. I stayed still for a few more minutes until I heard the knocks again and a male voice yell, "Police!"

I got up and walked to the door. It wasn't until I saw the look on the female officer's face that I realized that I was naked, dick slangin' everywhere.

"Sir, would you mind putting some clothes on?" the male officer asked. "A neighbor called and said she heard gun shots and saw a purple Grand Marquis speed off down the street. When they came back up the cul-de-sac, they got the license plate number."

"I'll be right back. Come on in," I told them.

I hated dealing with the police, but they were working for me this time. I was glad that we had neighbors who were concerned enough to call the cops, but I knew I wasn't gonna be elected Neighborhood Association President anytime soon with this kinda shit going on.

"What's goin' on, baby?" Tammy asked.

"The cops are here. One of the neighbors called them after they heard the gunshot. They say a purple Grand Marquis sped off only to turn back around and come back by. They got the license plate number. Whoever the hell it was wasn't smart enough to keep that from happening," I laughed.

"This ain't funny, Ty," she frowned at me and put on her silk robe.

"Where you goin'?" I asked her.

"To find out what the fuck is goin' on," she said, rolling her neck.

I laughed again. She wasn't playing with me. And I wasn't gonna be on the receiving end of the anger that was all over her face.

"Ok," I threw my hands up in surrender. I pulled on a pair of sweat pants and followed her into the living room where the police officers were standing.

"Have a seat, please," Tammy said, more as an order than a request. "Y'all want some tea or I can brew up some coffee."

"No ma'am," the female officer said, as she and her partner sat down at our dining room table.

"I'll take some tea," the male officer said, smiling a little too hard at my wife and watching her as she walked past.

I cleared my throat. Cop or no cop, I would catch a case if he didn't get his eyes off Tammy.

"So, what happened?" I asked them, looking at the shattered glass all over my living room floor. There was a brick laying on my sofa and it looked like it had a note attached.

The female cop's eyes followed mine and she got up and walked over to the couch and looked at the brick.

"Looks like you pissed someone off, Mr. Price," she said looking back at me. Her eyes traveled to my dick. What the fuck was the deal with these cops being straight up damn disrespectful.

Tammy came back with the tea and handed it to the male officer. "Here you are, Officer…"

"Smith. Sam Smith," he said and she laughed. He was looking at her like she was edible and I was about to blow when Tammy called him on the shit.

"Officer… Smith, is it? Don't you think it's disrespectful as hell to be looking at me like that in front of my husband? You're supposed to be here to help us and you're being really rude by the way you're looking at me right now."

I smiled. *That's my girl,* I thought to myself.

"My apologies, Mrs. Price… Mr. Price. It's just rare to see such a beautiful woman in this city. But you're right. I'll keep my eyes to myself and do my job," he said, looking like he was embarrassed. He should've been.

The look on his partner's face when he mentioned how rare Tammy's beauty was, though, had me about to burst out laughing. He must have been fuckin' her because she took real offense to that statement.

"So Mr. Price," she said with a whole lot of attitude, "do you have any idea who would do something like this?"

"No," Tammy answered for me. I could tell she'd peeped the way the officer was looking at me and was half a second from giving her ass a face check, too.

"I said *Mr. Price,*" the woman challenged her.

"I know what you said," Tammy said, standing up from her seat. "But I answered you. So next question."

"Was there any more damage?" I asked, knowing I'd heard gunshots, too.

"Yes, sir," Officer Smith spoke up trying to calm the tension, "your cars have been shot up. That's why my partner asked if you knew who could have done this. This seems personal. Especially if they got out of the car and threw a brick through your window with a note attached."

"Like my wife said, I can't think of anyone who would do some shit like this. I mean, I have an ex who may not be happy about us getting married. But, I don't think she would do something this stupid," I said, and Tammy cut her eyes at me. I could tell she didn't like the fact that I was taking up for Samantha.

"What's your ex's name?" the female officer asked.

"Samantha Johnson," Tammy offered before I could open my mouth. "Tell them her address, Tyrone."

I gave the officers Sam's address. The male officer had a smirk on his face that I wanted to knock off. Tammy was really in her feelings right now but I was gonna blame it on hormones. I knew she was just scared and wanted to find the people who had done the shit. The officers collected all of the information that we were going to give willingly and took pictures and the brick with the note as evidence. Then they gave us their cards and left. I went into the kitchen to get the broom and dust pan to clean up the mess that was in our living room. Tammy called Nel to tell her what had happened and that she and Ron needed to watch their backs. When she hung up, she had a worried look on her face.

"What's wrong, bay?" I asked, "I hope you aren't mad at me for saying Sam probably didn't do this."

"No. Nel said that y'alls momma is over there with some man named Samson that she's sayin' is her daddy."

"What?" I asked, getting heated.

"Yeah, says Tanisha just showed up with the man. Why would she bring some random man to her house like that? What's goin' on, Ty?' she asked.

I couldn't hear anything but sirens in my head. Tanisha had lost her damn mind. To bring a nigga to my sister's house, and Samson at that, was a complete violation. She'd better have a damn gun to her back or I was gonna end her life before that AIDS virus could.

"Tyrone," Tammy was saying, she was right in front of me now. "What's goin... *fuck*!!" she said and I realized she'd stepped on a piece of glass and her foot was bleeding.

I picked her up and carried her over to the dining room table, sitting her on top of it. I went into the bathroom and got some gauze and peroxide. The cut didn't look too bad. But I had to pull the glass out of it. She should have stayed her hardheaded ass away from the glass but I wasn't about to start that argument. After I tended to her foot, I went into our room to get dressed. I didn't care how much Tammy hated for me to run to my sister's rescue, this was one time I couldn't leave her to fend for herself.

Sheila

I hung up the phone with Tyrone with a smile on my face. I was gonna be an auntie. Leave it to Tyrone Super-sperm Price to get a woman who had been told that she couldn't have children pregnant. I looked over at Ron and knew that I was on the verge of losing him. I needed to be completely honest with him because I knew Delilah's ass was just getting started. I'd seen that spiteful bitch in action and I knew that if she was coming for Ron, she'd be coming for me soon, too.

"Bae, we need to talk," I said, tired of avoiding the subject anymore.

"I agree. We do," Ron said, sitting up in the bed. "What did you do to this woman to make her hate you so much?"

"Nothing, Ron. I swear. I thought she was my best friend. Then I found out that she was using me to get her foot in the door with this business venture, fuckin' my boss, *and* my man," I said, getting angry.

"You mean the married man you were dealing with?" he asked me, wanting to make sure I gave him every detail.

"Yeah," I said, "Anthony."

"The same Anthony who's a part-owner of the Mojo Lounge?" he asked, putting two and two together.

"Yes," I said as he started to shake his head.

"Wait..." he balled up his face, thinking, "isn't Anthony's wife the one who's paying you?"

"Yes..." I answered.

"Does she know you were fuckin' her husband?"

"Yes..."

"What's her name again?"

"Samantha... Samantha Johnson," I said, knowing what the next question was.

"What's the name of the chick Tyrone was fuckin' with who had an abortion?"

"Same woman," I confirmed.

"Wait... so, let me get this straight... you were fuckin' a married man who was knockin' down your supposed to be friend behind your back and your brother was fuckin' his wife? And you put the bitch yo' nigga was fuckin' and the nigga you were fuckin' with your brother whose wife the nigga was fuckin' together in a business venture?"

I laughed involuntarily because the shit sounded insane. If it hadn't happened to me, I'd probably be making the same face Ron was making right now.

"I don't see shit funny, Sheila," he said and I could tell he was mad as hell. "And you still working on this project with these insane motherfuckers? And brought me in on it and now I'm on some crazy bitch's radar?"

"Samantha paid me to do a job and I'm doing it. I don't let my personal life interfere with my business."

"That's fuckin' obvious," he said, getting up out of the bed and picking his clothes up off the floor.

I was trying to think fast to find something to say before he walked away for good.

"Bae, wait," I said, trying to get out of the bed.

Before I could say anything else, I heard my alarm chime.

"Comin' in," I heard Tanisha's voice coming from the kitchen.

"Hey, Momma. We're in here," I yelled.

"*We*?" she asked. "Who's we? Are you decent, child?"

"Yeah, we'll be out in a minute," I said, my eyes pleading Ron not to leave.

He looked at me and just shook his head. I knew he loved me and that was my only saving grace right now. I was grateful, too, because I was definitely in love with him and would probably just give up if I lost him because of Delilah's crazy ass.

"I'll stay, because I know you need me to. But we gone have a serious ass talk," he said and I felt like a little kid in trouble with her daddy.

"I'm willing to talk about anything that will keep you here with me. I really am sorry about not telling you all this. I didn't think that crazy bitch was still on the shit she's on. I thought when she got outta jail, she was gonna gone about her damn business."

"She's still a partner in the business, isn't she? So how the hell you figure that? I swear you book smart as hell but your common sense is that of a damn toddler," Ron said, and, even though it hurt, I knew he was telling the truth. My lack of common sense had been getting me and my loved ones into shit the majority of my life.

We both started walking towards the door leading to the living room. I was in front of Ron, but when I got to the door, I stopped dead in my tracks.

"Nel, what the hell is wrong with you?" Ron whispered in my ear before looking over my shoulder and seeing the man standing in the living room with Tanisha.

"What the fuck is *he* doin' here, Tanisha?" I asked, feeling myself start shaking.

"Is that any way to greet your father?" Samson said, a sly smile on his face.

Before I could say anything, my cell phone rang. I ran to answer it and was excited to see Tammy's face on the screen.

"Hey Tammy, what's up, sis?" I asked, figuring she was calling me to tell me she was carrying my nephew.

"Nel, you at home?" she asked in a tone that made a chill come over me.

"Yeah, I'm on bedrest, where else would I be?"

"Look, somebody in a purple Grand Marquis came over here and threw a brick with a note through our living room window. Then they shot up our damn cars. We don't know who did it but I need you to keep your eyes and ears open. You might wanna go stay at Ron's for a while."

My eyes were fixed on the door so I only heard part of what she said. Something about a purple Grand Marquis and police. The rest was just mumbles.

"Nel... NEL, did you hear what the hell I said?" she yelled into the phone.

"Hmmm?" I said, absently into the phone.

"What the hell is wrong with you? You ok?" Tammy asked me.

"Tanisha's ass is over here and she got some nigga here that's claiming he's my daddy. I remember him. His name's Samson and he was the pimp who was trickin' my momma out. I thought he was locked up... or dead. But his ass is standing in my living room right now," I said just above a whisper.

Ron was still standing in the doorway but he had his back to the living room and was watching and listening to me. There was a tired expression on his face and I felt like this was gonna be the nail in the coffin of our relationship.

"Got damn it, Sheila Penelope Price! Do you fuckin' hear me?" Tammy yelled again into the phone. "Me and Ty will be right there," she said and hung up the phone.

I sat on my bed, not wanting to face Tanisha *or* Samson. I knew if I went in there right now, I would cuss Tanisha's ass slap the fuck out. I knew I couldn't trust her ass. What the fuck good did it do to bring her former pimp around me? And then he was claiming to be my damn daddy. She'd brought some bullshit, and dangerous bullshit at that, to my house. And in my mind, that made her as bad as Delilah.

Ron walked over and sat down beside me on the bed.

"You can't win, can you, bae? You're like a fuckin' drama magnet," he said, shaking his head. "I ain't goin' nowhere so let's find out what the hell he's over here for."

I nodded weakly and laid my head on his shoulder. I was definitely grateful for him. He was really showing his loyalty today. He patted my thigh and we got up from the bed. I was gonna try to get to the bottom of this before Tyrone got here and acted a whole fool.

Samantha

I didn't know what the fuck Kris was into but I was pissed. I didn't know who to go the fuck off on first, him or Tyrone. I remembered Tyrone had changed his number so I would get Kris's ass first. I stormed down the hallway and beat on the door to the spare bedroom. I didn't care if he had a bitch in there, her ass could get whooped the way I was feeling right now.

"What the fuck you beatin' on my door like the cops for, Samantha," a barely awake Kris came to the door.

I punched him in the mouth and went to swing again but he grabbed my hand and turned his head to the side like I was crazy.

"Why the hell are the police comin' over here accusin' me of vandalizing Tammy and Tyrone's house, Kris?" I was livid.

"I don't fuckin' know. Probably because your little boyfriend told them that if anyone was gonna do some dumb shit, your spiteful, manipulative ass would be the one to do it," he said, struggling to keep me restrained.

"And you don't know shit about that, as usual, right?"

He looked at me and didn't answer, which was answer enough for me.

"Kris, I don't know what you and your psycho bitch Delilah got goin' on, but I'm about sick of the embarrassment of having the got damned cops coming to my door. It's not enough you got some bitch in my house like she supposed to be here, now this shit. I just can't win with you. Do you remember your children live in this fuckin' house?" I screamed, hot tears running down my face.

"I told you I don't know what you're talkin' about, Sam. You better chill the fuck out before the cops end up back here, carting your ass downtown for assault and battery. I know you got cameras all over this damn house, so proving it wouldn't be too hard. Then I'd be able to fuck who I want where I want 'cause you'll be sittin' your ass in a cell somewhere," he threatened, making me calm down.

He was right. After all the shit that had gone down, I'd had surveillance cameras installed all over the house. The data was streaming to a cloud that was maintained by the security company. I was the only one with the passcode, but a subpoena was all that it would take to obtain the footage.

"Fine, Kris, you win. Let me go," I demanded.

"You got some nerve talkin' about what I'm doin' when, before I ever brought a bitch in this house, *where our children live*, you were fuckin' Tyrone's ass in our bed.

And *who* brought *their sister* Delilah in the house? And don't think I don't know about you fuckin' Beth in here. I'm not deaf, dumb, or stupid. You walk around here like you're the damn victim when you're as bad, if not worse, than me."

He looked at me one more good time before letting me go. He knew me so well because he knew I wanted to knock him in his shit again. I stood there, mad as hell and embarrassed. Then I looked behind him and saw the same hoe in his room that had been there the other night. She must mean something to him because he was willing to bring her in this house over and over again. I looked at him with tears in my eyes and my pride tucked between my legs. I turned to leave, still talking big money shit.

"Whatever that bitch Delilah is into, you better not be involved. I won't be there to bail your ass out this time."

"While you're over here threatening and accusing me, you might wanna call your lil' white girlfriend and ask her ass what she and Delilah got planned for yo' ass," he yelled at my back.

I paused for a moment before keeping it moving. I went into my room to nurse my bruised ego. A few moments later, I heard that bitch moaning. I knew she was doing the shit on purpose. I turned on the TV and put on Pandora's Mary J. Blige channel on full blast. My mind kept going back to what he said about Beth and Delilah. Even though he may be lying, I was gonna find out for myself.

*****

The next morning, I called Beth and asked her to meet me at Starbucks for coffee. She agreed and I got there half an hour early so I could get a spot in the back and got my phone ready to record our conversation. I was gonna send a copy to my new attorney and ask him to send it to the police if anything happened to me. I couldn't trust any-damn-body. I felt defeated. But, if something *did* happen to me, I wanted to make sure Kris, Beth, and Delilah's asses were charged for it.

Beth walked in and I stood so she could see me. She made her way to me, limping, her face grimacing in pain. She had on big sunglasses but I could see that her lip was split and she had a big purple bruise on her cheek that she'd tried to cover up with makeup. My anger quickly turned to concern. I wondered what the hell happened to her. I couldn't deny that I loved her, even if she was triflin' as hell.

"Hey, Beth," I said, my voice filled with sympathy. "What happened to you?"

"Delilah happened to me," she said as we sat down. She shifted around in her seat, trying to get comfortable.

"What the hell..." I asked, getting angry. Then I remembered why I was there. I pretended to check my phone for a text message and turned the recorder on my phone.

"Look, Sam, I'm pretty sure I know why you called me here. Me and Delilah and Anthony were planning on taking you for every dime you had. We know about all the cameras, hell, I was there when you had them installed. I know your password and Anthony has a lawyer who was gonna file for divorce and use the recordings of me and you as evidence. Anthony had the camera in the room disconnected by having Dee call in and pretend she was you when you were at work. There's no proof that he's been fuckin' that girl Keisha that he plans to marry as soon as you're out of the picture. He was gonna take you for everything, the house, the kids... everything. I know the shit was foul but, well," she paused and pulled her glasses off, showing one of her eyes swollen shut, "this is what happens if you don't do what Delilah says."

"Why are you telling me this now?" I asked, curious about her change of heart.

"I went to see Tre, you know, the dude who used to fuck with Delilah and was Tammy's boyfriend who got locked up for beating her ass, shooting her, and drug possession."

"Yeah, I know Tre," I said, urging her on.

"He warned me that Delilah was dangerous and told me that her daddy used to fuck her and that she killed her momma. Said she burned the house down with her momma in it and went to the psych ward. He told me that she was gonna kill me once I served no purpose to her no more," she explained.

"And you believed him?" I asked, kind of skeptical.

"My momma used to tell me to always trust the information, regardless of who it's coming from," she said. "And then, when I got home, *this* happened," she said, pointing to her face.

"Damn, baby," I said, my face wrinkling up.

I knew about Tre and about Delilah getting locked up for burning the house down with her mom asleep in it. I even knew about the accusations that her daddy, my daddy, used to molest her. Tuskegee was a little ass city. Everybody knew everybody else's business. I sat there, deep in thought, looking from my hands to Beth's face. I didn't know what to do.

"So, I understand if you don't want to fuck with me anymore. You can't trust me. Hell, I wouldn't trust me after all this shit," Beth said sadly, her one open eye filling with tears. She flinched like it hurt to cry and I reached over and took her hand.

"Look, Beth, what you were planning to do was fucked up. But, well, is this the first time she's put her hands on you?" I asked.

"No. This is just the first time that it was this bad," she confessed.

"Well, you were making decisions to try and survive. You were loyal, just to the wrong person. Do you think you could be loyal like that to me?"

"Sam, I love you. I just know you're still in love with Anthony *and* Tyrone. I don't wanna be third in line. But yes, if given the chance I would love you with everything in me," she said, rubbing the back of my hand with her thumb.

"You're not third in line. Those men never wanted me. Hell, Kris got mad at the fact that I was with you and we were enjoying each other so much. You're being honest with me right now and that means something in my book. You just can't lie to me again. Can you promise me that?" I knew I was being stupid to trust Beth, but I really did love her. And in a way that I had never loved another person. I would die for her. Without question.

"Yes Sam, I can promise you that. I *love* you," she said and I leaned in to kiss her split lips.

"Now, what did she do to you and where's Tre? I've got a proposition for him," I said, tapping my phone again to turn off the recorder.

Anthony

I had no idea what the hell Delilah's ass wanted with the keys to my repo lot, but I should've known that it was gonna be some stupid shit. She'd taken one of the cars we'd repossessed and gone and vandalized Tammy and Tyrone's house. This bitch was reckless. She didn't care about how her actions effected anyone else. That purple Grand Marquis could be traced back to me and she hadn't had enough damn sense not to choose a more inconspicuous vehicle or park somewhere away from their house when she went throwing a brick in the window and shooting up their cars. I had to cut her ass off before I ended up in jail and me and Matt lost the business. My phone rang. I looked down and saw that it was Matt.

"Kris, what the fuck, man?" he said as soon as I answered. "The cops are here and they're checking our lot and searching our logs. Where's the purple Grand Marquis we had here? They said it's been involved in some kind of vandalism. They're shutting us down until this case is solved, nigga. If you don't tell me what the hell is goin' on, I'm gone come pay your ass a visit, brother-in-law or not," he threatened.

Usually I didn't take kindly to threats but I couldn't blame him for bein' mad. I needed to find out what had happened to that car. And what the hell Delilah had done. I walked Keisha out, giving her a kiss and a smack on the ass.

"What's wrong, baby?" she asked, her forehead wrinkled.

"Nothing you can help with. Some shit is goin' down and I need to get over to the shop ASAP."

"Well, let me know if I can help with anything," she said with a smile. "Wait, is this about the purple Grand Marquis that was seen in that vandalism case? Are you involved in that, Anthony?"

"Yeah... well no... but your coworkers are there going through our records as we speak so I need to get down to the shop," I explained as best I could.

"That's my case," she said, frowning up at me. "You need to tell me what the hell is goin' on so I can see what I can do to help."

I stood there, contemplating telling her the truth but decided against it until I was able to find out what was going on.

"Look, you need to get to work and I need to get to the shop. I promise I'll tell you everything when we go to dinner tonight. And I don't want you cleaning up my messes and jeopardizing your job. I'm the man in this situation, even if you do carry a gun. Let your man handle his own shit, ok?" I said, pulling her in for a kiss and grabbing two hands full of her ass.

"Ok, but if you need me, you better call me."

"Yes, Misses Officer," I smiled, wanting to take her ass back in the room and dick her down again. But I had to get down to the shop before the shit hit the fan. I was seriously thinking about killing Delilah's ass and sparing all of us a whole lot of misery.

Tyrone

When I heard the name Samson, I was ready for war. I was young when my mother met him but I remembered what he did to her. How he used to beat her and turn her out. How he put us out on the streets right after she had Nel. I thought he would die in prison but I guess I thought wrong. Tammy was on my heels, getting dressed. I didn't want her there but I didn't have time to argue with her ass, either. We walked out to the garage and got into the pink Expedition I bought her as a wedding present. As girly as Tammy was not, she loved the color pink and I'd gotten this truck custom painted with the pink flip-flop. The only reason this one hadn't been damaged this morning was because it was in the garage.

Even though it was her truck, I hopped in the driver's seat. I pulled out of the driveway, maneuvering around our damaged cars, and headed to my sister's house. I drove carefully because my wife and unborn son were in the car, even though I wanted to run every light and stop sign on the way there. When we pulled up, I turned off the truck and looked over at Tammy. She looked frightened.

"What's wrong, Tam?" I asked.

"I don't know. I just gotta bad feeling about this."

"Well, if you want, you can stay in the car."

"Then who's gonna keep your ass and that hot ass temper of yours under control?" she said smiling.

I couldn't help but smile back. She knew me so well. I got out and ran around to open the door for her. I helped her out of the truck and we walked up the walkway to Sheila's house. The door was unlocked so we walked in to find what looked like a standoff. Ron was holding my sister while she sobbed uncontrollably. Tanisha was looking lost and Samson had this smug ass look on his face.

"The fuck is goin' on here," I asked, making everyone turn in our direction.

"Ty, Tanisha says this is my daddy. Is that true?" Nel asked, never letting Ron go.

Ron looked tired. He'd been through enough drama with the Price family to last him a lifetime, but I had to commend the man for still being there trying his best to console my sister.

"What are you talking about?" I asked, looking back and forth from Tanisha to Samson.

"Samson is Sheila's daddy," Tanisha said, looking at me with apologetic eyes.

"Ok, but why are you here right now? What are you trying to do? You bring this nigga to her house when you know she's battling cancer. You don't know what he's capable of and now he knows where she *lives*. I swear I'm starting to see that you're gonna be more of a liability than an asset, Tanisha. What the hell is the matter with you?" I yelled across the room.

Tammy put her hand on my arm, trying to calm me down, but I was thirty-eight hot. Tanisha looked at the floor. I could tell she hadn't thought that shit out.

"Ron, let me take Nel in her room so she can lay down and you four talk," Tammy offered, walking across the room towards them.

Samson watched her as she walked, making me even madder. I was already ready to snap his neck for turning my mom out and onto drugs then leaving us in the streets. Now he was here, in my sister's house, upsetting her when she was already sick. And he had the *nerve* to be eyeballing my wife.

"Put your eyes back in your motherfuckin' head, Samson. I'll kill one over that one," I said through clenched teeth.

"Hell, I would, too," he said smiling nonchalantly but taking his eyes off my wife.

"What do you want?" Ron asked, coming back into the room looking like he was ready to take both Samson and Tanisha out.

"Delilah," Samson said sitting down on the arm of the sofa.

"Delilah?" Ron and I asked at the same time.

"Yeah, Delilah," he repeated.

"Yes, baby..." Tanisha said walking over to him.

"Not you. They know what I'm talking about," he said, dismissing her.

An even more confused look came over her face.

"How do you know we know where she is?" I asked, sitting on the arm chair facing him.

"I know everything. Just because I was locked up doesn't mean I don't know what's goin' on. So... where is she?"

"She???" Tanisha asked, her face balling up like she'd just come to some conclusion that no one else knew about.

At this point, I didn't care. She'd crossed a serious line bringing this man here. But I would handle her ass another time. I was curious about why he wanted to find Delilah but knowing her ass there was no telling what she'd done to him. I looked at Ron and shrugged. He wasted no time telling Samson where Delilah lived. Even wrote the address down for him. I laughed to myself because I knew he was partially glad that he wasn't gonna have to get her handled. It looked like Samson had it out for her ass.

"Who's Delilah?" Tanisha asked, not trying to hide her anger.

"She's my daughter," Samson said in a tone that let her know that was all he was going to say about the situation.

I cocked my head to the side because I knew I couldn't have heard him right. Because if Delilah was Samson's daughter and Tanisha was saying that he was Nel's father, then that meant that Delilah, Samantha, and Sheila were all *sisters*. I was glad I was sitting down because that shit would've knocked me down. We all sat there in silence, letting it sink in. Ron was looking around, a bit confused. I would fill him in later. Poor guy.

For the first time, I took a long look at Samson. I could see it. Sheila had Tanisha's eyes and lips but she had his nose, build, and skin color. Samantha had his eyes and nose but must have had her mother's lips, build, and color. Delilah had his whole face. She looked just like the man.

I stood, keeping my eyes at Samson.

"You got what you came here for, so y'all can leave now," I said and Ron squared up like he was ready to turn with me if it came down to that.

"And you ain't got no need to come back here, either," he added, making it clear that he wasn't gonna have Sheila upset anymore.

Samson laughed and stood up from his seat on the arm of the couch. He was all of six-feet-five inches. If Samson wasn't his real name, it sure as hell was a perfect nickname for him. His locs were sweeping the floor.

"Ain't no need for all that. Like you said, I got what I wanted. I won't bother Sheila anymore. I know she's sick but this was an urgent matter and I needed the information that only y'all had."

He walked out the door with Tanisha right behind him. She looked back at me and I just shook my head at her. Some people never changed. She was showing me that she was one of them. I was officially done with her ass. I hoped Nel was, too.

When we heard them pull off, Ron looked at me for an explanation.

"Samson is Sheila, Samantha, and Delilah's father. They're sisters," I explained.

"Wait, the Samantha you used to fuck wit'?" he asked, trying to make sure he understood.

"Yep. Sam knew she and Delilah were sisters. Her mom was Samson's mistress and Delilah's mom was his wife. Seems like he had mistresses all over the place," I shook my head.

"Well, I don't care who that nigga is to Nel, he need not bring his ass back over here," Ron said angrily.

"I don't think he will. Whatever he wants with Delilah was the only reason for him to be here. Come smoke with me," I offered.

Ron looked like he'd been waiting on that invitation all night. We walked out and sat on Sheila's patio furniture. I lit up a Newport and he lit up a Black.

"So, you serious about my sister, huh?" I asked him. I know he'd said he was before, but I really wanted to make sure all this shit hadn't changed his mind.

"I am... I was... is it always this much drama with her?" he asked and I laughed.

"Welcome to the Price family," I said, blowing out smoke and laughing.

"Man, this shit is too much to handle. I don't know if I want this kinda drama in my life. I love your sister, but all of this other shit, I can't deal, man," he said, honestly. I had to respect his honesty because Tammy felt the same way and she'd been around us for years and years.

"Look bruh, I feel you. This is a lot to deal with. Tanisha just came back into the picture. Nel really did think that Delilah was her friend and had no idea she was her sister. Samson's ass got locked up not too long after he put me, Tanisha, and her out on the street. And she didn't know Anthony was married. She's just naïve and too trusting" I summed up what he'd experienced in the past few days.

He laughed. I looked at him because I didn't think I'd said anything funny.

"What's funny?"

"I just told her today that her ass has no common sense. She's a genius and an idiot at the same time," he said, laughing again.

"Yeah... yeah she is," I said, joining in with his laughter. I didn't like him calling my little sister an idiot, but some of the choices she'd made had me feeling like there wasn't any other word for it.

"Is shit gonna calm down 'round here?" he asked seriously.

"Once we get Delilah's ass off the streets, yeah, I think so," I said. "But, with Nel being sick, that's gonna be an issue in and of itself."

"I can deal with that. Her being sick ain't a problem for me. I just want this outside shit to gone somewhere."

"I feel you," I said, nodding my head. "Somebody threw a brick through my window and shot up mine and Tammy's cars."

"What the hell? You think you know who did it?"

"Yep... Delilah. This shit has her name written all over it. I was actually gonna get with you and get her address myself tomorrow, but Samson beat me to it. I'm pretty damn sure he's gonna handle her and anybody else that's associated with her ass, so I'm just gonna lay low and watch the shit unfold."

"Man, I just don't wanna be anywhere near that fallout," Ron said, getting up and putting his Black out on the bottom of his shoe. "I'm finna go check on my baby. You and Tammy staying here tonight?"

"I don't know, it may be safer for all of us if we do. Just in case that fool comes back to our house or Samson or Tanisha brings their asses back over here."

"Let's go see about our women," Ron said and dapped me up.

I was really starting to like him. He was down for my sister and that wasn't something that I had seen or she'd experienced. But that's what happens when a man chooses a woman. And it would be nice to have somebody to kick it with that wasn't Tammy or Sheila. As long as Nel didn't get caught up in anymore dumb shit, I may have myself a new brother-in-law sooner or later.

Delilah

I walked up the walkway to my house feeling great! I'd fucked up Tammy's and Tyrone's cars and thrown a brick through their window with a note attached that looked like it came from Samantha. The car I was driving would be traced back to Anthony and once they were locked up, what proof would they have that I'd done it?

"Hey there, Sweetness," I heard a voice coming from the shadows.

I didn't want to turn around because I didn't want to acknowledge his presence or that he'd found me. I knew Beth wasn't here because she left to stay with her dad after I kicked her ass the other night. Now, I wished I hadn't because there was no one there but me... and him. I thought about turning and running but I knew he would catch me. He'd find me, just like he always did. Just like he had this time. I wondered who'd sold me out. Someone had to have told him where I was. Whoever it was would have hell to pay.

"So, you gonna let me in or what?" he asked walking up behind me.

I wanted to muster up the strength to tell him no but I knew better. He'd beat my ass and probably rape me right out here in the open. I twisted the key and opened the door. I didn't know what I was gonna do, but I was gonna have to think fast. Samson walked into the house like he owned the shit. He sat down on the couch and patted his lap.

"Come sit on Daddy's lap. We gotta lot of catching up to do," he said smirking and licking his lips.

"I'm too old to be sitting in your lap, Samson," I said, not budging.

"Say what now?" he asked, moving like he was about to get up. I flinched instinctively. All these years later, all the shit I'd done without fear or a care in the world, and he still scared the life outta me.

Samson laughed and leaned back. He unbuckled his belt, then unbuttoned his pants. He unzipped his zipper and looked at me like he was waiting for something.

"Well come put your head in my lap, then," he ordered.

I still didn't move. I wasn't that little girl he used to make suck and fuck him every night when he came home from being in the streets. If he was going to violate me, he was gonna have to take it from me.

He stood up, pulling his pants and shoes off. He stared at me, massaging his dick. The sight of it disgusted me. I didn't know what I was gonna do and was mad as hell at myself for not hitting him in the head with something when he bent over to take off his pants and shit. He did it slowly, deliberately, like he was daring me to do something. I watched him watch me and get himself off, squirting all over my floor. When he finished, he sat his bare ass on my couch.

I didn't know what to say or do. I wanted to go get my gun but knew he'd never let me get that far. So I stood there staring at him. I was trying to figure out what this hold was that this man had on me. I eyed him as he pulled on his boxers. Never taking his eyes off me.

"What do you want, Samson?" I asked, sounding a lot more confident than I felt.

"You better check your fuckin' attitude before I come over there and stick my dick in your mouth," he stood and threatened.

"Do you hear yourself? I'm your *daughter*, motherfucker! What kinda fucked up wiring do you have that you think it's ok to say some shit like that to your child?" I yelled at him.

I was hysterical. He'd really lost his mind, if he had one in the first place. I was ready to blow his fuckin' head off. I started to walk towards the bedroom. He was gonna get the hell out of my house or lose his life tonight. He took one step over with his long legs and blocked my path.

"Move, Samson," I squared up with him.

"I ain't movin' shit. I know that look. You 'bout to do something stupid so let me save you from yourself. Go sit ya ass down before you make me remind you who the hell I am," he said, a smirk coming across his lips.

I wasn't gonna move but I knew that as crazy as I was, he had me by about thirty degrees of insanity. And that was before he was locked up. I started to back up, moving towards the arm chair. He didn't move or take his eyes off of me. If he'd blinked, I would've been in the kitchen ready to carve his ass like a pumpkin. I sat in the chair and his smirk turned into a full-on grin. He knew he still had me under his control. Feeling beaten, I decided to find out what he wanted from me. I'd kill him another time.

"What do you want from me, Samson?" I asked, my tone so soft I almost didn't recognize my own voice.

"That's more like it," he said and laughed loudly. "I want what's mine. Your little friends owe me money and you owe me for the last twenty years I spent in prison because of your ass. So, you decide how this is gonna go. You need to tell me where them lil' niggas Tre and Scooter at, and don't lie to me 'cause I know you know. And then we'll talk about what you owe me."

"Samson, I don't owe you nothin'. You were havin' sex with your daughter. That's wrong in everybody else's mind but yours. I'll tell you where Tre and Scooter are at, but I want that to pay my debt. If you'll leave me alone, I can take you to 'em right now," I said, knowing I was sellin' Tre and Scooter out but willing to do anything to get Samson to leave me alone.

"It ain't that easy, Sweetness," he said looking me dead in the eyes. "You mine so, whether you wanna accept it or not, you ain't gettin' rid of me!"

Before I could say another word, there was a booming knock on my door.

"Samson, open this fuckin' door! I know you in there!" A woman's voice screamed from the other side.

I rolled my eyes, all this damn noise was gonna get Beth's ass evicted from this bourgeoisie ass complex. *Oh well, not my problem*, I thought to myself. I was snatched from my thoughts by a woman's scream. Just that quickly, Samson had walked across the room, opened the door, and snatched her into the house, slamming the door behind her. He had her by the throat up against the wall, her feet dangling, slapping her with his free hand. She wasn't a very attractive woman, heavier set with platinum blonde hair, a big nose and full lips. She had on clothes that were way too young for her. There was something about her eyes that seemed familiar to me but I couldn't put my finger on why.

I wanted to run in their direction but I was afraid of Samson turning his anger on me. All I could do was watch in fear like I did when he used to beat the hell out of my mom when I was growing up. I saw her eyes start to roll back in her head and realized he was about to kill her.

"SAMSON!" I yelled, walking over and placing my hand on his shoulder. "Put her down," I said, calmly.

He looked at me, his eyes wild with anger. And then, just like when I was younger, they softened. He dropped the woman and she landed, roughly, onto the floor. He looked at me and pulled me to him. My skin began to crawl. I don't know why I could get him to calm down when others couldn't and why he'd never laid an angry hand on me. Lustful, yes. Angry, no. It was unsettling.

The woman struggled to catch her breath. He pulled me to him, his lips inches away from mine. If it was any other man, I would have loved to be held like this, but this was my *father*. It was unnatural.

"See, nobody else makes me feel like this," he said. "You mine, Delilah."

"Samson, let me go. You and this woman need to get outta here. Neither one of you are supposed to be here. Y'all done caused enough disruption for the night. Come back by tomorrow and I'll take you to Tre 'nem," I said just wanting to get away from him.

I felt metal press against my temple. I looked at Samson with tears in my eyes.

"I don't know why you think I'm stupid, Delilah. I ain't goin' nowhere. Now, go sit yo' ass down before you make me hurt you."

I didn't hesitate this time because I knew that Samson wasn't joking when he pulled his gun out. I walked over to the arm chair and sat down. I didn't flinch or look back as I heard him hit the woman over and over again until I heard her stop making a sound. I assumed she'd passed out at that point. Samson walked past me towards the bathroom and I heard water running. He came out wiping his hands on one of Beth's decorative towels. His gun was tucked visibly in his waist.

"Who is that?" I asked as he sat down on the couch facing me.

"Tanisha," he said as if that was explanation enough.

I stared at him blankly waiting for more information and he gave me none. He got up and went into the kitchen to get himself a beer. Sitting back down, he looked at me like I was the crazy one. He took a swig of his beer and his expression started to turn angry.

"Clean that shit up," he said like he used to after he'd beat the hell out of my mom.

Over twenty years later and he was acting like I was supposed to know what to do and, in reality, I did. I got up and went to the linen closet and got some towels and cleaning supplies. I sat the woman that my father had referred to as Tanisha up against the wall and used my body weight to pick her up off the floor. I carried her into the spare bedroom and laid her down. Her lip was busted and there was a gash on her temple where he'd hit her over and over with the gun. Her breathing was shallow and I said a silent prayer that she didn't die in my house.

I walked back into the living room and cleaned the blood off of the hardwood floor and the wall. When I was done cleaning, I threw the towel in the trash. I felt myself getting sick. It was my teenage life all over again. I put Samson away because of what he'd done to me and killed that pathetic ass bitch of a mother because she was weak and decided to fuck my man because she was mad that I'd fucked hers. Can you believe that shit? She was actually mad at me for fuckin' her husband like I was sleeping with my father willingly. I ran to the bathroom and threw up until there was nothing left in my stomach.

When I walked out of the bathroom, Samson was no longer in the living room. I heard the TV from my bedroom and my stomach began to churn again. I walked to the door and saw him, laying in his boxers, in my bed, watching TV like he was supposed to be there. He looked over at me and patted the bed beside him. I stood, stiff as a board.

"Don't make me get up," he said cutting his eyes at me.

I walked into the room and sat on the other side of the bed. I laid down fully clothed and hoped that he would just let me go to sleep.

"Show daddy what he's been missing," he said, his eyes glued to the screen.

With tears in my eyes, I pulled back the covers and did as I was told.

Tre

"Nigga, have a seat. You been pacing since Dee left here," Scooter yelled at me. "You makin' me nervous."

"You need to be nervous, too. You know we fucked Samson out of a quarter mil when he got locked up. We ain't got the money for this man when he comes to collect, so he's gone take our *lives*. I need to gone get Tammy so we can dip!" I said, still pacing.

"Delilah told us not to do nothin' 'til we hear from her," Scooter said rolling a blunt.

"You think she ain't gone turn on us? That bitch ain't got no loyalty. Especially when it comes to Samson. That nigga beat and raped her into submission years ago. I don't trust her. He probably already got to her ass. We sittin' ducks in this room. We gotta move!"

My mind was racing. I didn't know what I was gonna do or where I was gonna go but I knew I needed to make a move. Then a light bulb went off. Samantha was Delilah's sister and Samson's daughter. She had money and she was gonna get us out of this shit. I knew she had kids. I just needed to get some info about where they were. Beth was gonna be my way to them. I just had to decide how to play it. First, I had to go see Tammy. She thought she'd gotten away from me but she was mine, married or not, and she was coming with me.

"Man, I know that crazy look. What you over there schemin' on?" Scooter asked, lighting his blunt.

"I know how we gone get Samson's money and the money to get the hell outta dodge," I said, walking over to take the blunt he was passin' to me.

"Ok, I'm all ears," Scooter said sitting back in the chair, his arms crossed across his chest.

I know he was skeptical because he thought I was crazy for still thinking Tammy was gonna come with me. But he couldn't talk because his ass wanted to run to Florida after his skank ass baby momma even though she cleaned his ass out and ran to some nigga she met on Facebook.

"We gone take Samantha and Anthony's kids and hold 'em for ransom. They negligent assess so busy fuckin' around on each other that I don't see it being too hard to do. And then, when we get our money, we gone break Samson's ass off and grab Tammy and we're off to Florida," I said, as if the plan made perfect sense.

"I thought so," Scooter laughed, shaking his head.

"What you thought? And I ain't say shit funny," I got mad.

"You done lost your whole fuckin' mind, man. You talkin' 'bout kidnappin' kids and shit. And you need to let Tammy's ass be. She ain't comin' nowhere with us and that nigga Tyrone will search 'til his death for her. All the pussy in the world, all these hoes you done knocked down, and you won't let Tammy ass go. You need to leave that girl be and accept that you lost," he said, laughing again.

"You ain't accepted you lost," I shot back knowing that would piss him off.

"My bitch got my kids. You ain't got no ties to Tammy. She don't want you. Let sleepin' dogs lie."

"Man, fuck you. Look, you in or not?"

"Man, why can't we just kill Samson and Delilah's asses and gone 'bout our business. You know we got a lil' stash, so why make our shit hot?"

"Nigga when you become a bitch?" I asked shakin' my head at Scooter.

"I ain't no bitch, but I ain't stupid, either. You a glutton for punishment. You know what the fuck Tyrone gone do to you if you come for his wife. You just can't seem to get that shit through yo' hard ass head. I'm startin' to think you like him whoopin' that ass. You do what the fuck you wanna do. I ain't tryna get locked up or killed with yo' ass. I'm out," he got up and walked towards the door.

"You'll be back! You ain't shit without me and you know it," I said making him turn around and look at me.

"You wanna know what I am without you that I won't be if I keep rockin' with yo' stupid ass?" he asked, laughing, "ALIVE!"

He opened the door and walked out. I knew he was done. He would be on the first thing smokin' to Florida in the morning. Let his ass go. I didn't need him. He was dead weight anyway. His baby momma had him so whipped that he wasn't thinkin' straight.

I sat planning my next move. I needed money, more than that ten stacks a piece that Scooter had hidden from his baby momma because as whipped as he was, he wasn't all the way stupid. I wanted some real money and I needed Samson off my back. But I wanted to be able to take Tammy somewhere that Tyrone wouldn't find us because, as much as I hated to admit it, if he did my ass was as good as dead. I was more worried about him than I was about Samson. Samson really wanted Delilah and if she could get him another cash source, he wouldn't be too worried about us.

Don't get me wrong, he was still comin' for us, well me, because I was his right hand when he got locked up. But it was more an ego thing than it was about the money. I had to plan this shit out. Had to get Beth to go along with me kidnapping her girlfriend's kids.

I needed to see Tammy. I missed her. I treated her like shit but she didn't know how to stay in her damn place. If she would've just let me do me and held down the house, we would've been cool. But she had to fall for that nigga Tyrone. Sneaking and writing him and going to see him and shit. She was fraternizing with the enemy. She deserved every ass whoopin' she got because of it. But now she'd married the nigga and was pregnant. All the time we'd been together, all the years I shot up in her, and she never got pregnant. Made me wonder if she was on birth control so she wouldn't have my baby.

I hated that nigga Tyrone. He got everything I couldn't. His sister worshipped him. Tammy was in love with him and pregnant with his seed. Made me wanna kill his ass. I decided to make that my first order of business. That way when I took Tammy, I wouldn't have to worry about him coming looking for her. I grabbed my keys and headed out to find Tammy. I figured she would be at Sheila's house since I'd heard about Delilah's stupid ass shooting up their new house.

I laughed at Delilah. She truly hated anybody that was happy when she wasn't. She had no off switch and that made her more dangerous than it made her an asset. I needed to take care of her ass, too. I knew she was gonna sell me out to Samson, if she hadn't already. There was no tellin' what she was gonna do next.

*****

I drove down Sheila's street slow as hell. I was in a rental so no one would know it was me but I wasn't gonna risk it. I was just in time because Tammy was getting in her car. She was looking damn good in her yoga pants and tank top. She'd put on some weight, but it was all in the right places, and her hips were spreading. I followed her to Target. When she parked and got out of the car I made my move. I walked over to her truck and punctured the driver's side tire. Then I sat waiting for her to come out.

Thirty minutes later she walked out, all smiles. She had bags in her hands and I could see that she'd bought some little boy clothes. I felt myself getting jealous. She was giving this nigga a junior. That was supposed to be *my* baby! That's ok. Once we were outta here, I was gonna fill her ass with my babies. I watched as her facial expression changed when she saw her tire was flat. She looked down into her purse searching for her phone. I took my opportunity.

Jumping out of my car, I jogged over to her. She was still looking in her massive Michael Kors handbag so she didn't see me coming.

"No need to call that nigga. Your knight in shining armor is right here," I said walking up so close to her that I could smell her perfume.

"Tre! What the fuck are you doin' here?" she asked, so startled that she dropped her bags. She reached into her purse again.

"Don't be stupid, Tammy. I know you probably got some mace or a piece in that purse. Don't make me hurt you," I threatened, making her take her hand out of her purse.

"What do you want?" she asked with more attitude than I liked.

"Yo' man ain't here to protect you so you might wanna adjust your motherfuckin' tone. Don't act like you forgot who the fuck I am. And stop lookin' around, these white soccer moms ain't gone help you, either."

She stood there staring at me. I grinned feeling like I was winning.

"I just wanted to come and offer my congratulations. You all married and shit and now," I said looking at the bags on the ground, "it looks like you got a bun in the oven."

She stood silently, still not saying anything. I liked it that way. I could smell the fear coming off her. Her phone started to ring. She looked down at her purse and back up at me. I gave her a glare that dared her to answer it. She didn't. It rang again. She looked like she was about to cry. I was loving the hold that I still had over her. She was stuck. Her tire was flat and she knew that I would beat her ass and purposely stomp that baby out of her stomach if she tried me.

"That nigga hella insecure the way he callin' you," I smiled, taking every opportunity to talk shit about Tyrone.

"Tremaine, what do you want from me? I'm married now. I'm about to have a family. I need you to tell me why you're following me and why you fucked up my tire. I got shit to do. You're wasting my time," she said getting bold.

"If we wasn't in public, I'd slap the shit outta you. You better be glad..."

"Do you need some help, Miss?" A woman walked up interrupting us. I didn't see her come from behind me and didn't know how much she'd heard.

"Yes, my tire's flat and I need to call my husband. Can I use your phone because I can't seem to find mine?" Tammy said relieved that the woman had interrupted us.

"Sure," she said, reaching into her pocket and pulling her phone out.

Tammy looked at me and smiled. I didn't like that shit but wasn't about to handle her with a witness present.

"I'll see you soon, Tammy. Just know you're not untouchable. We'll be a family again real soon," I said, walking away.

I got in my car and sped off mad as hell at the interruption. I was gonna have Tammy if it killed me. An, knowing Tyrone, it just might.

Tammy

Tre showing his ass up at Target scared the hell out of me. I thought he was still in jail and not only was he out, but he'd found me and slashed my tire. He was outside his mind if he thought that I was gonna be with him. I'd kill myself first. I was grateful for the woman who came up when she saw the fear in my face. There had been ten before her who looked at me and then looked away, picking up their pace. That shit made me angry. They could have at least called the cops or gone back in the store and told a manager that there was a woman in trouble.

"Thank you so much," I said handing the woman her phone back after I'd finished talking to Tyrone.

"I know that look. I used to have an abusive husband and no one would help me. I saw your bags on the ground and your eyes pleading for someone to help you and I just couldn't leave. My conscience wouldn't let me."

"You're a godsend. All those other women kept walking like they didn't see me. I wish there was some way that I could repay you..." I said waiting for her to tell me her name.

"I'm Imani... Imani Jones. And you don't owe me anything. Someone did the same thing for me. Just be careful. I'll stay here until your husband gets here just in case that fool is still somewhere watching us."

We laughed and talked about nothing in particular until Tyrone came flying into the parking lot like a mad man. I knew he was pissed when I told him that Tre had flattened my tire and harassed me at the store. I didn't know how he'd found me but I knew Ty was out for blood. When he got out of the car he rushed over to me, completely ignoring Imani's presence.

"You alright?" he asked, kissing me and placing his hand on my stomach protectively.

"Yeah, bay. Thanks to Imani, here," I said, smiling at her.

"Thank you so much," Tyrone said looking at Imani with grateful eyes. "If you hadn't helped her, there's no telling what may have happened."

"You're welcome. Well, it was nice meeting you, Tammy," she said, taking her leave.

"Thank you so much again, Imani. I'm gonna come check you out at that poetry reading," I yelled behind her.

"Cool, you got my number," she said waving and walking to her car.

I was gonna buy her dinner or something. She'd saved my life, *literally*.

Tyrone wasted no time getting the spare out of the truck and starting the tire change. He was ready to get me the hell out of this parking lot and the way he was acting, the hell out of this city. I couldn't blame him. I sat in his truck while he changed my tire. He'd gotten it repaired while we were staying at Nel's. I felt bad about how frightened and frustrated he was. I knew it was because he didn't want anything to happen to me or the baby and after our cars and house being shot up, Samson showing up at Nel's, and now Tre finding me at the store, he felt like a failure when it came to protecting his family.

"Gone get in the truck and I'll follow you to Nel's house," he said his face filled with anger.

"Baby, you can't protect everyone. Shit happens and people are crazy. Please don't beat yourself up about this," I frowned.

He didn't respond. I got out of his truck and into my own headed back to Nel's house. I was worried. Not about Tre coming for me, but because I knew that my husband had about had enough and was about to snap!

I had to figure out a way to calm him down before he went on a rampage, combing the city until he found Tre's ass. I didn't want him to go back to jail. Our son and I both needed him.

Tanisha

I woke up with a banging headache in a room that was unfamiliar to me. There was a woman sitting at the foot of my bed staring at me. I sat up with a grunt and she moved closer to me. I looked around and realized I wasn't at home.

"You ok?" she asked.

"My head is killin' me and I feel like I been hit by a damn freight train. So, I'd have to say no," I said not meaning to be sarcastic but I felt like she had something to do with me feeling the way I was.

"You weren't hit by a freight train," she laughed dryly. "You were hit by a Samson," she said, making the memories from last night come back to me.

"Who are you?" I asked her.

"My name is Delilah. I'm Samson's daughter. He's been molesting me since I got my first period. He came here last night and you were right behind him beating down the door like the police. I figure you're the girlfriend, huh?" she asked me.

"I thought so," I said, "but now I'm not so sure."

"The only person Samson has ever been devoted to, aside from himself, was me. Not that I wanted him to be. I never understood what kinda mis-wiring he had going on that made him think it was ok to have sex with his daughter," she said, pouring her heart out to me. "You look so familiar. Do I know you?"

"No honey, I don't think so. Where's Samson now?" I asked looking around.

"He's in there sleep. He'll be up in a little while so maybe you oughtta get outta here before he gets up."

"You should come with me. He's dangerous, look what he did to me," I wanted to save this girl but she seemed like she was stuck.

She shook her head 'no'. "He'll find me wherever I go. There's no point in me trying to run anywhere. You see he found me here. There was no way that he should've been able to do that. But Samson has eyes and ears everywhere," she said sadly.

I wrestled with whether I should tell her that Ron was the one who told him where he could find her or not. I wanted to help her and make her feel better, pointing out that if she hadn't drugged Ron she wouldn't have been found, but I knew that would put Ron and Nel in the mix of this mess all over again. As bad as I felt for Delilah, I needed to protect my own children. And how was I to know that she was being honest with me? I had to stop trusting everyone who came to me with a sob story.

I looked at her sadly. I felt for the child because I would hate for Sheila to feel like she seemed to be feeling. Instead of telling her about Ron giving Samson the information, I decided to offer some motherly advice.

"Look Darlin', if I can't get you away from here, I just want you to know that you don't have to be abused like this. You need to get help. Samson is obviously too far gone but you, honey, you're too beautiful a girl to go through this. I have a daughter with Samson and I swear, if I had found out that Samson was touching Sheila like that the cops wouldn't have been able to get to us before I killed his ass. She and I have just started to reconcile and I wouldn't let her go through anything like this. I really wish you would let me help you."

Delilah's head turned to the side when she heard Sheila's name. I smiled with pride even though my mouth hurt like hell because I realized how well-known my baby girl was.

"I wasn't the best mom and my children had a really hard life because of some of the choices I made. But I wouldn't want them to end up in a situation where they felt they had no way out. I don't know where your momma is, but I know that no decent mother would want this life for their child," I said easing out of the bed so that I could get out of there before Samson's ass woke up.

"Tanisha..." Delilah said, staring at me blankly.

"Yes?"

"Is your last name Price?"

"Yes. Yes, it is," I said, smiling and turning to her to see she was standing right in front of me with a butcher knife in her hand.

"You're Sheila and Tyrone's mother, aren't you?" she asked, a smirk on her face.

I didn't understand what was going on or get the chance to answer. She stabbed me in the stomach. I fell to the floor feeling a burning sensation where she'd shoved the knife. I could feel myself losing blood. Delilah came to stand over me, a deranged look in her eyes and a smirk across her lips.

"It's nothing personal. I don't know you. But I know your children. You mean nothing to me but you said y'all are reconciling so yeah, you're gonna help me make them pay for thinking that they can send me to jail and go on with their lives like nothing happened."

"Delilah! What the fuck!" Samson asked rushing into the room and leaning down, pressing his hand against the open wound.

"You got your enemies and I got mine," she said, nonchalantly. "We both got some vendettas to settle. You want me to help you with yours, you help me with mine."

Samson looked between me and Delilah. I could tell he was torn. I thought that was crazy given the way he'd whooped my ass last night but I guess he didn't want me dead. He was just trying to get me under control. It was hard for me to breathe. I was trying my best to hold on but I felt myself getting weak. I closed my eyes to the sound of Delilah and Samson arguing. He was pissed that she'd stabbed me. She was upset that he was so angry over me. The last thing I remember was the feeling of being lifted. I didn't know if it was my soul leaving my body or them carrying me out of the house. Either way, shit wasn't good.

Sheila

I was cuddled up with Ron watching *Dusk 'til Dawn: The Series* on Netflix when my cell phone started ringing. I didn't want to answer it. I was trying to chill and relax and enjoy my time with bae but it could have been an emergency.

"Hello?" I answered without looking at the caller ID.

"May I speak to a Miss Sheila Price," a woman's voice came over the line.

"Speaking," I said, pulling the phone away from my face to see a number that I didn't recognize.

"Miss Price, your mother has just been brought into the Emergency Room. She's been stabbed. You were listed as her next of kin and her emergency contact on her cell phone..."

"What hospital did you say you were with again?" I asked getting out of bed and walking over to my dresser to pull out some sweats.

"Jackson Hospital, ma'am."

"I'll be there shortly," I said ending the call.

"What's goin' on, bae? Who's in the hospital?" Ron asked, concern all over his face.

"Tanisha... my mom... she's been stabbed," I explained putting my shoes on.

"You can't go up there! Your immune system is compromised. You just had chemotherapy, Nel. I know you're worried about Tanisha, but you have to take care of yourself first," he said walking over to block my path. "Lay down."

"Ron, I have to go. That's my mother and she needs me."

"You know who needs you? Jeff. Tyrone and Tammy and your little nephew that's on the way. *Me.* I need you, Sheila. And I'm not gonna lose you because you keep trying to rush to help grown ass folks. Please get back in the bed," he pleaded.

"Ty!" I yelled to my brother.

He and Tammy were still staying with me because of the shit that had happened at their house. He came running into the room.

"What's wrong?" he asked, standing in front of us in nothing but his boxer briefs and socks.

I couldn't help myself, I burst out laughing. My brother must have been on high alert to come running like that. Poor guy. His nerves must've been shot.

"Ain't shit funny, Nel. What the hell you hollering my name like you lost your damn mind for?"

"I'm sorry. You just... you just..." I was trying to get my words out but I was laughing too hard.

"Bruh, the hospital just called. Tanisha been stabbed. Nel thinks that her weak bodied ass is going somewhere but she got another thing comin'. I guess she called you in here to see if you could go see what's goin' on because I ain't lettin' her go nowhere," Ron explained while I composed myself.

"Stabbed?" Tyrone asked, like he hadn't heard right.

"Yeah," I said finally composed, a smile still across my lips. I knew this wasn't the time to be laughing but I really was tickled at my brother's entrance.

"So you want me to go up there. I don't know if I wanna be bothered. After that shit with her bringing Samson in here, I really don't care much to be involved in Tanisha's life. I mean, I don't mean her no ill will but I'm not gonna break my neck for her. I got my own child and a wife to think about and you..." he said looking at me and shaking his head.

"I tried to tell her ass," Ron chimed in.

"Nel, you need to lay yo' ass down. I mean it!" Ty yelled at me. He rarely raised his voice at me so I knew he was serious.

I slid my feet out of my shoes and climbed back into the bed. I wasn't up for a fight and with Ron and Ty tag-teaming me, I knew I didn't have a chance in hell of getting out of this house.

"Are you gonna go check on her, Ty?" I hoped he'd say yes.

"Man, I'm going my ass back to bed. We got enough drama and bullshit goin' on in our own lives, Tanisha needs to handle her own. Maybe this is karma for some shit she did in the past," my brother said walking towards my bedroom door.

"She's our mother, Ty," I used his own words against him. "I wanted to pay her ass off and send her kickin' but you wanted to try and get answers and shit. Now look where we are. There's no such thing as Tanisha's mess. Her mess is ours and vice versa."

"I'll go in the morning."

"What if she needs us before the morning?"

"There ain't shit we can do for her that the doctors and nurses will have been able to handle before we get there."

I let out a deep sigh. I was outnumbered. I wasn't testing Ron or Tyrone. I was too weak to be taking my ass anywhere near a hospital and I knew it. They were right. So as badly as I wanted to be there for Tanisha, I knew that my health was more important because I have a child of my own to worry about.

"She's in Jackson Hospital, Tyrone," I said, getting in the bed and laying with my back to him and Ron to let them know I was pissed.

I said a silent prayer that everything would be ok before closing my eyes and drifting off to sleep.

Tyrone

I walked back into Nel's spare bedroom and got in bed with Tammy. I didn't feel bad for Tanisha. I really did feel like it was karma catching up to her that had gotten her stabbed. And with her being involved with Samson, there's no telling what had led to the shit. Either way, I wasn't gonna worry about it until the morning. I had bigger fish to fry. Tre was out of jail and harassing Tammy. I was tired of having to protect my family from these motherfuckers. From Samson to Delilah to Anthony to Tre, I had about had my fill of Montgomery and all the drama this city held. But I couldn't leave my sister while she had cancer. I had to admit, though, short of Samson, Sheila was the reason that any of these folks were in our lives.

I mean I don't regret meeting Tammy, which wouldn't have happened if Nel hadn't gotten pregnant by Tre, but the rest of 'em I could live without. I didn't even want to be a part of the business venture anymore. I'd do my own thing. I had a good job, I didn't need to be in business with people who were reckless and could possibly do some shit that would have me locked the hell up.

"Everything ok?" Tammy asked, rolling over and kissing me on my forehead. She always did that when my forehead was wrinkled with worry.

I relaxed my face and smiled at her. That woman's touch was magic. I loved her with every fiber of my being. I figured I owed it to her to be honest and wanted to get her take on the entire situation.

"Tanisha's in the hospital. Apparently, Nel is listed as her next of kin. Can you believe she was trying to get her stubborn, sickly ass up to go to the hospital? I told her I'd go in the morning. I'm not really feeling going to check on Tanisha after the whole Samson situation yesterday. I feel like whatever happened to her, she brought on herself. Am I being cruel?" I asked, waiting on her to give me her thoughts.

"I get it, baby. You're fed up with all of this drama and anyone attached to it. Tanisha is your mother but she wasn't the best mother to you or to Nel. She's only been back in our lives for a short time so, I can see you not really wanting to even be involved with her and her shit. But, and I'm playin' devil's advocate here, what if she dies? How would you feel then, knowing that you're acting out of anger and frustration? If you can say honestly that it wouldn't bother you, then we can roll over and go to bed and go to the hospital in the morning. But, if you'd feel guilty, then we need to get up and get dressed and go see what the hell is going on," she said reading my face.

"Come on," I threw the covers back and got up to get dressed. She was right, I wouldn't be able to live with myself if something happened to Tanisha and I wasn't there. And I knew it would eat Nel alive, too.

Tammy got up and started getting dressed. I watched her, smiling. I was the luckiest man alive. I had this beautiful woman who loved me unconditionally and she had agreed to be mine forever and was now giving me my first child. Thinking about it, I was kinda glad that Samantha had the abortion. I didn't want to be attached to her, Anthony, and their drama any more than I had to be. Sam and Nel were sisters, but they didn't have to be around each other. I didn't see any family reunions in their future, especially since Nel had slept with Sam's husband.

"Boy, why aren't you putting yo' clothes on? What you over there thinkin' about?" Tammy asked pulling me back into the moment.

"You and how amazing you are. How blessed I am to call you mine and how, if that nigga Tre shows his face again, I'm gonna kill his ass with my bare hands," I said honestly.

"Bay, don't worry about Tre. His ass is dead on sight. If he comes around again you won't have to do him nothin', I owe his ass for years of abuse anyway," she said, a look I'd never seen coming across her face.

I put on my sweat pants and a t-shirt and grabbed my keys. I didn't disturb Ron and Nel telling them we were leaving. I figured they were enjoying some alone time or already asleep so I'd just give them an update in the morning. We got in Tammy's truck and headed to Jackson Hospital. When we got there, the receptionist told us that she was in ICU and had just gotten out of surgery.

"Surgery?" I asked, concerned.

"Yes, sir. She was brought in by ambulance. She was found on the side of the road on I-85. If a Good Samaritan hadn't called 911, she would have bled to death right there," the receptionist said.

"That doesn't make sense. If she was bleeding like that there was no way that she could have driven herself," I was confused and frustrated.

"That's the strange part and the thing that made the person call. They saw a woman putting Ms. Price into the driver's side of the car before hopping into a car with a man," the receptionist gave us all the information she knew about the situation.

"Thank you so much, can we go see her?" Tammy asked, her hand resting on my forearm trying to calm me down.

"Sure. I think there are some cops in there with her right now but they should still let you see her."

When Tammy and I walked into the hospital room, after arguing with the damn nurse trying to tell her ass that we were relatives, we saw that Tanisha was conscious and not alone. There were two police officers there and he doctor. They looked at us oddly when we walked in.

"Hey Tanisha, how you feeling?" Tammy spoke first.

"I'm ok. I guess. As ok as I can be," she said, weakly.

"Good," Tammy said, before turning to the others in the room. "I'm Tammy Price. Tanisha's daughter-in-law," she said extending her hand to the officers.

"Yes ma'am, Mrs. Price, Officer Smith and my partner Officer Keisha Taylor," the male officer said,

"Wait, I know you," Tammy laughed.

I took my eyes off of Tanisha long enough to realize that these were the same two cops who were working the case dealing with our house being vandalized. We'd never gotten the female officer's name but I remembered that nigga because of the way he'd been eyeballin' my wife.

"Isn't this an interesting coincidence," I finally spoke up.

"Can we speak with you and Mrs. Price outside, Mr. Price?" Officer Taylor asked.

"Sure," Tammy said, leading the way out into the hallway. I followed and the officers were right behind.

"Look," Officer Taylor said getting right to the point, "your mother gave us a statement. She said that a woman named Delilah Powell stabbed her and that Delilah and a man named Samson left her for dead on the side of the highway. The reason we wanted to talk to you all is because the name Delilah Powell also came up in our investigation into the vandalism of your house and your cars being shot up."

"Do you know this person and have any idea why she wants to kill your mother and shoot up your house?" her partner asked.

"Because the bitch is unstable," I said angrily without thinking.

"What my husband is trying to say," Tammy said, stepping in front of me and pulling my arms around her resting my hands on her stomach, "is that we know Delilah. She and I were friends in college. We lost touch but reconnected not too long ago. I found out that she was sleeping with Ty's sister's boyfriend and severed ties with her again. She just got out of jail for beating Sheila, Ty's sister, up in her own house. They're also in business together, a venture that they forged before anyone knew just how unstable Delilah was."

"This boyfriend that Delilah was sleeping with, what was his name?" Officer Smith asked.

"Anthony Bailey," I offered. "His wife Samantha is the ex-girlfriend that I'd mentioned would be one of the people who would want to shoot our house up."

Officer Taylor had a look come over her face like she was about to be sick. I could tell she knew Anthony or Samantha, or both.

"Wait, so you and your sister were sleeping with husband and wife and the husband was also sleeping with this Delilah person who beat your sister up, went to jail for it, and now she's shooting up your house and cars and stabbed your mother?" Officer Smith said, his head turned to the side. "Where are the cameras? This shit needs to be on TV!"

"I don't see anything funny about this," Tammy checked his ass. I swear I love my wife.

"My apologies, I know this is a serious matter. It's just almost too much to believe. Do you know where we can find Ms. Powell? And do you know the man that she was with? Your mother said his name is Samson?" Officer Smith asked.

"My sister's boyfriend knows where to find Delilah. I'll call him and get the address that he has for her. And Samson is Delilah's father. He just recently got out of jail as well," I said, walking away to call Ron.

He answered sounding like he was getting some good sleep.

"Hey bruh, what's up?" he asked, sounding like he was sitting up in the bed.

"I'm up here at the hospital with Tanisha and there are some cops here. They say that Samson and Delilah are the ones who stabbed her and left her for dead. What's the address that you have for Delilah?" I asked, getting to the point.

"That bitch is a fuckin' menace, man. Normally I wouldn't help the cops but if it means taking her ass off the streets so we can sleep easier, I'm all for it. Hold on, lemme get the address from my texts. I'll forward the shit to you," Ron said. I could tell he really wanted to lay hands on Delilah himself.

"Alright, thanks man. Hopefully they'll get her ass," I said knowing Delilah was probably already in the wind.

"Here's the address we have for her," I said, walking back over and holding my phone up so that the Officers could copy the information from the text that Ron had just sent me.

"Thank you for your cooperation, Mr. Price," Officer Taylor said weakly. Something about her entire demeanor had changed.

"Don't thank me. Get that psycho-bitch off the streets before somebody ends up dead," I grabbed Tammy's hand and walked back into Tanisha's room to talk to her doctor.

"Is she gonna be ok?" Tammy asked the doctor as soon as we got into the room.

"She lost a lot of blood and we have to take special care because of her condition, so it'll be touch and go for the next couple of days. She needs her rest, but I know you want to speak with her so I'll give you a few minutes," the doctor advised.

"Thank you," I said shaking the doctor's hand.

"How are you, Tanisha?" Tammy asked walking over to the side of the bed.

"As ok as can be expected, given the circumstances," she replied with a weak smile. I could tell she was in a lot of pain.

"Delilah did this to you?" I wanted to get as many details as possible.

"Yeah. I told her I was Nel's mom and she walked up and stabbed me. I don't remember much else other than Samson and her arguing before I passed out. They left me for dead," she said crying.

"Calm down, Ma. I need you to calm down. Did you tell her anything else about us? About Nel? She just stabbed you like that because you said you were Nel's mom?" I tried trying to make sense of everything.

"Is that so hard to believe, Ty?" Tammy asked, being the voice of reason. She was right. Delilah didn't need a reason to do some evil shit.

"Naw bay, I guess it's not. That bitch is vile," I shook my head.

"Look, Ma, I need you to get better. Nel is about to lose her mind. We almost had to strap her ass to the bed to keep her from coming up here with her weakened immune system. She really wants to keep you around and we'd love for our son to meet and get to know you, too."

"Awwww, Tammy you pregnant?" Tanisha asked, smiling as broadly as her body would let her.

"Yes ma'am," Tammy beamed.

"Well, I guess I need to hurry up and get outta here so I can get ready for this new grandson of mine, huh?"

"You better," I said leaning down and kissing her on the forehead. "We're gonna get outta here. Call me, not Nel if you need anything. She needs her rest, ok."

"Ok, I promise," Tanisha rested her hand on mine. "Now you get your wife home. Don't be stressin' my grandbaby."

"Yes ma'am," Tammy said as we left the hospital.

Walking out, I called Ron again and told him to be on full alert. There was no telling what Samson and Delilah would do next.

Anthony

I opened the door for Keisha. She'd called me as soon as she got off work and sounded like something had her shaken up. She walked in and past me without saying a word. She went straight to the bedroom and sat down on the bed. I walked in and was about to sit down beside her but the look she gave me froze me in my tracks.

"Close the door, Kris," she said, throwing me off because she never called me Kris.

I walked back over and closed the door. Samantha was out of town with Beth so I didn't know why she was so worried about the door being open. I was more concerned with the look that she'd given me. When I turned back around, she was crying.

"What's going on, Keisha?" I asked her, walking over to her.

"So, are you using me?" she asked.

I was completely confused about what she was talking about. I stood there trying to figure things out. Finally, I gave up and asked her.

"Using you for what, baby? I don't know what you're talking about."

"You *know* the woman who took the car from your repo lot, the same woman who shot up and vandalized the Price's house, and who stabbed your ex-girlfriend Sheila's mother."

"Sheila's mom has been stabbed?" I asked, that bit of new information sticking out to me.

"Yeah, so I'm asking this question again. Are you using me?"

"Keisha, how could I be using you? I didn't know you were a cop when I met you. And how in the hell could I have known that you were gonna be the one on these cases? Montgomery is just small as hell, baby. But no, I'm not using you."

"Did you sleep with Delilah Powell?" she asked, looking me straight in the eyes.

"Yeah, I did. I slept with her while she and Sheila were friends."

"So you were cheating on your wife with Sheila and on Sheila with Delilah. What kinda trife ass nigga are you? And now you're fuckin' me, in your wife's house, sometimes while she's here. I believed you when you said y'all were getting a divorce, but now I'm not so sure," she said.

"Look Keisha, I know this shit is looking bad. But I was just stupid with my dick. I haven't been with anyone but you since I met you and I swear I've never felt the way that I feel when I'm with you. If you want me to leave this house and get my own to prove it to you, I will. If you want me to file for divorce, I will. But don't hold my fucked up past against me. Delilah is insane. And she's dangerous. I gave her the key to my lot but I didn't know what she was trying to do. She threatened my children. They know her. She said that she would take them if I didn't go along with her. And, I mean, look at what she'd done to Sheila and what you just told me she did to her mother. Would you test her crazy? I sent my kids to my mom's house for a while just to keep them safe until I could figure out what to do with her."

"Kris, this is a lot. I mean, my job could be on the line if they find out I'm sleeping with you. I didn't mean to catch feelings for you. You were just something to do. But it's turned into something so much more. You wanna show me you're serious? Yes, move out of this house. And stop fuckin' your wife. And yes, get a divorce. I think we need a break until we find Delilah and get her ass off the streets."

"A break?" I asked making sure I heard her right.

I heard the rest of it and was willing to do it for her. Keisha had my head gone. She was beautiful, the sex was amazing, and she was smart. I wanted to be with her and would do anything to show that.

"Yeah, I really like you and want to build with you. But no one is worth my career. And to be honest, if Delilah knows where you live, you'd do better to get outta here as soon as possible. She doesn't know Tanisha survived the stabbing yet, but when she does, she's gonna be looking for somewhere else to hide out. Tyrone said she and Samantha are sisters and this guy, Samson, is their father and fresh out of jail. She'll probably come this way next," she said, her face full of concern.

"Well, if I came to your house, you could be my bodyguard," I smiled, flirting with her.

"You can come for the night, but you gotta find somewhere else to go tomorrow," she said, blushing.

I could tell she was really feeling me. I was glad because I could actually see myself being with her and doing right by her. I started packing a bag. I would get a hotel room tomorrow. I needed to lay low until Delilah's crazy ass was locked up for good.

Getting in the car, I followed Keisha to her house. I called Beth on the way. I felt like I owed it to her to warn her and Sam about what was going on.

"Hello," she answered, sounding stressed.

"That's no way to sound when you're on vacation," I teased, trying to lighten the mood.

"What's up Anthony?"

"You and Sam need to be careful. Delilah is on the rampage. She stabbed Sheila's mom and I got a feeling she's coming for one or both of you next," I warned.

"Why would she come for us and not for you?"

"I can't say that she won't come for me but I'm getting the hell out of the way for a while. I'm gonna get the kids, too. So tell Sam I'll call her tomorrow and tell her where we're at. You two need to be careful. Her, well her and Sam's, dad is out of jail and him and Delilah together can't be a good mix. They may be coming after Sam and her money next. So, y'all just watch your backs, ok? I gotta go," I said ending the call as I parked in Keisha's driveway.

She walked into her house and I followed. Her home was nice. She gave me the tour and I put my bag on the floor in her bedroom while she went in the kitchen to heat up some leftovers for us. She came in with a tray holding two plates of chicken parmesan, a glass of wine, and a Budweiser. We climbed in bed, ate, and watched World's Dumbest Criminals until we dozed off. There was something so comfortable about being around Keisha. I would get a hotel, pick up my kids, and get with my attorney first thing in the morning.

Samantha

I walked out of the bathroom and heard Beth on the phone. We'd taken a trip to N'awlins to get away from all of the craziness that was going on back home. The fun had been short-lived though, because she'd gotten a call from her rental office saying that there'd been a disturbance at her house and when the manager had gone into the apartment earlier today, there'd been blood in the living room and the spare bedroom. Now she looked like she'd just gotten some more bad news. I didn't know how much more of this I could take.

"What's up, babe?" I asked sitting on the edge of the bed putting on lotion.

"That was Anthony. He said Delilah stabbed Sheila and Tyrone's mom and that she had linked up with your dad. Said he's out of jail," she summarized the conversation.

"Samson's out of jail?" I asked, fear filling my voice.

"Your dad's name is Samson?" Beth asked, stifling a laugh.

"Yeah, that's why he named her Delilah and my mom named me Samantha," I explained. "What else Kris say?"

"That they'll probably be coming after you and your money next and that he's gonna get the kids and hide out tomorrow," she filled me in on the rest of the conversation. "He said he'll call you tomorrow to tell you where they're at."

"Ok," I said, my mind racing.

My mom had told me stories about Samson. He was ruthless. And the fact that he'd molested Delilah showed me that he wasn't wrapped too tight. I was honestly afraid for my life. I knew I needed to get back so that I could get to my kids. I knew Beth needed to get back to find out what was going on with her apartment, too. She wasn't in a hurry though, because Delilah had beat the shit out of her and I know she's scared of her, too.

"What we gone do, baby?" Beth whined, coming and laying up under me.

"I don't know. I guess we need to get a hotel room too, until something breaks. I mean, I'm sure the cops are looking for her if they know she stabbed Sheila's mom. I just wonder how she even got to that girl's momma. I swear poor Sheila can't catch a break," I said really feeling bad for her.

I was tired. I wanted to just pack up and leave and never come back to Montgomery. But I had kids and couldn't just leave them like that. I knew they were as much in danger as the rest of us. And my mind was really reeling about the fact that Samson was out of prison. I had never met him and hadn't planned on it. But the money that my mom had left me wasn't a secret so that made me a target. I scooted back in the bed, my back rested against the headboard. Beth crawled up on the bed and joined me. She rested her head in my chest and I could feel her heart racing. I wanted to say something to calm her down but there was nothing that could be said. Both of us knew our lives were in danger.

I settled in my head that we would head home tomorrow. I was going straight to the police station to see what, if anything, they could do to protect me and Beth. Then we'd get some clothes and find out what hotel Kris was staying at with the kids and get a room there, too. At least if all of us were together, we could team up if the time came to fight. Or maybe it would make us all sitting ducks. How did I know that Kris wasn't in bed with Delilah? I watched Beth as she drifted off to sleep. I wouldn't worry her with the thoughts that were running through my head. We'd strategize on the way home in the morning.

Ron

Tyrone had me on high alert. He called me when he and Tammy were leaving the hospital and told me that Delilah had been the one who'd stabbed Tanisha. I didn't say anything to Sheila, just took the safety off my piece and made sure that the alarm was on. I was ready to defend my woman and her house. I was grateful that Jeff spent most of his time with Nel's foster mom so he wasn't caught up in all this bullshit.

I sat on the couch where I had a clear view of both doors. I hadn't told Nel about the job offer I'd gotten in Atlanta but I was seriously thinking of taking it and taking her and Jeff with me to get them the hell out of this fucked up city. I didn't know if she was willing to leave her job but I figured she could open an office for them in Atlanta since she said they'd been talking about branching out, anyway. Hell, with the money I'd be making, she didn't have to work at all. But I knew her better than that. I'd come with the branch out suggestion first.

I'd tell her about all of this when shit calmed down. Right now, I needed her to get healthy. That was my primary focus. And keeping her safe until they got Delilah off the streets. I heard the alarm chime and looked to see Tyrone and Tammy walking into the house. They turned on the lights and Tammy screeched.

"Ron you scared the shit outta me," she said.

"My bad, sis," I said, getting up from my seat on the couch.

"Gone to bed, bay. I'm gonna sit here and talk to Ron for a few," Tyrone said, patting Tammy on the ass.

"K," she said without hesitation. I could tell she was tired.

When she was out of the room, Tyrone went back into the kitchen and came back with a bottle of Petrón and two shot glasses.

"Man, thank you for rockin' wit' my sister. I know you walked into this clusterfuck. I really appreciate you," he poured us both a shot.

I took mine to the head before I spoke. I liked Tyrone and wanted to be honest with him. I wanted his take on my plans.

"I love her, bruh. I think she could be Mrs. Roberts. I wanna get her and Jeff out of this city, though. I got a job offer in Atlanta and want to take them with me. I wanted to get your thoughts on it, though. You know Nel better than anyone," I put it all out in the open.

"Wow," he said, taking his shot. "You wanna know if she'll come with you. Hmmm," he said like he was thinking.

"Yeah, I was thinking of suggesting that she open a branch of Vantech in Atlanta because I know she ain't the housewife type."

"You'd be asking her to leave everything she knows," he said. I could tell that he was still thinking. "But a change of scenery would be good for her. I'm planning on getting out of the business venture for the Lounge myself. I don't wanna be in business with Delilah and Anthony."

"Yeah, I think Shawn can handle the marketing for the Lounge from this point. I know her bosses were thinking of branching out, so I don't see why she shouldn't be the one to do it. We could start over. I wanna ask her to marry me," I confessed.

Tyrone poured another round of shots. He threw his head back, taking his time before saying anything. I didn't know if that was a good thing or a bad thing. But I would wait to hear his thoughts.

"I don't doubt that you love my sister. I mean, you staying around after all of the shit that's happened, the way you've been by her side through her chemo, and even now, you sitting here standing guard over the house shows me that your feelings are genuine. I just don't know how she's gonna take being asked to leave Montgomery. I mean her foster mom is here and now Tanisha. This is her *home*."

"If it was Tammy, wouldn't you wanna take her away from all of this bullshit, though?"

"Yeah, I would. Hell, I'd thought about taking her away from this shit now, so I get how you feel. I just don't know how she's gonna take it, for real," he took another shot.

"How who's gonna take what?" Sheila asked standing in the doorway to her bedroom.

"What are you doing outta bed?" Tyrone and I asked at the same time.

"Don't flip this on me," she laughed. "I rolled over and you weren't there, Ron. And then I come in here and my two men are taking shots and speaking in hushed tones. So, is it me or Tammy that y'all are talkin' about?" she asked, coming over and sitting in my lap.

"You..." Tyrone said, getting up from his seat and walking towards the spare bedroom. "I figure you two need to talk."

"Talk about what?" Nel asked looking me in the eyes.

"Well, there's a lot that we need to talk about. First of all, what if I said I wanted you to be my wife?" I asked, giving her the good news first.

"Stop playin' bae," she stifled a grin.

"Who's playin'?" I asked. I wanted to wait until I got a ring and planned something romantic but with the way things were going I wanted to get it done as soon as possible in case some shit popped off with Delilah.

"Are you serious?" she screeched.

"Dead ass."

"I'd say yes. Without a doubt!"

"Good. Now... I got a job offer in Atlanta. I would be running the marketing department for Jive Records. I want to take you and Jeff with me," I said watching her face to see how she felt about it.

She sat there silently, caught up in her thoughts. I couldn't read her facial expression. I hoped that she wouldn't shoot it down without talking about it first.

"You could talk to the other executives about opening a branch in Atlanta. Or... you could be a housewife and let someone take care of you for once," I said, hoping to sway her. "Shawn can handle the marketing for the Lounge. I think you've got too many personal ties to that job and getting away from that Lounge and the parties involved would be good for you and for your health."

"Baby, you're asking a lot," she furrowed her forehead. "I mean, my whole life is here..."

"So is so much pain," I pointed out, cutting her off. "From your childhood to Tre and now Anthony and crazy ass Delilah. Baby, you need to get out of this city. I love you and I'm worried about you. I want you to be ok."

"Awww. I love you, too. I'll think about it. But my answer hasn't changed about marrying you so, I guess I'm kinda saying that I'll be moving to Atlanta soon. I mean, I have to go where my husband goes, don't I?" she smiled.

I let out a sigh of relief. I wanted to marry her and didn't want to fight her about the move but I would have left her if I had to because I was gonna take that job.

"So, when do you leave?" she asked.

"Six weeks," I told her.

"I guess I need to schedule a meeting with the executives, huh? And with Shawn so that I can pass the job onto him. I need to tell Tyrone too, since he's part owner of the Lounge," she planned her next moves. "And talk to my foster mom and Jeff about the move. We need to get him registered for school out there."

"I'm glad you're serious about the move. I was worried," I admitted.

"You only find the love of your life once. I'd be stupid as hell to let you go," she said, smiling and kissing me on the cheek. "Hey, did Tyrone say anything about Tanisha? I know they went to see her."

"Yeah, he said Delilah was the one who stabbed her. That bitch is crazy. You need to be careful," I said, realizing that Tyrone hadn't given me any real details on how Tanisha was doing. "Let's get some more rest and we can ask him in the morning."

"Ok, Mr. Blowemup," she teased getting up and walking towards her bedroom.

I got up and followed her. I was so happy that she was gonna be my wife. That I was gonna be able to get to be a male role model for Jeff. And that we would be able to get the hell out of Montgomery. I hadn't been here that long but, with all the drama that had happened recently, I couldn't get the hell away from here soon enough.

Tre

I had to flirt my way into another room. The buck-toothed clerk was gonna come see me after she got off. Hell if I fucked her just right, I could get the room for free. She told me Scooter had checked out. I knew his bitch made ass was gonna run. I wasn't gonna be so easy to scare off, though. I was gonna get Samson before he got me and then go get my woman and leave. I'd let go of the idea of kidnapping Sam's kids. That shit would be too much work to do on my own.

"Hello?" I answered my phone, not recognizing the number.

"Still slick with that mouth of yours, I see," Samson laughed on the other end of the phone.

"Samson, what's up, man?" I tried to hide my fear.

"My quarter mil is what's up. You got my money or are you gonna pay your debt with your life?" he threatened.

"You know I ain't got that money. My girl took that shit when I was locked up and Scooter's girl took the rest of the stash and dipped to Florida"

"Y'all always were weak for pussy. I done already got Scooter 'cause he ain't have my shit. You're next," Samson said, letting me know Scooter was dead.

"Look man, I told you I ain't got it. Can't we work somethin' else out?" I tried to bargain with him.

"You need to get that bitch of yours to give you back what's mine. That's the only thing we can work out. You got two days or I'm comin' to see yo' ass," he said before hanging up the phone.

I looked out the window to see if I could make Samson out because I was sure he was watching me. I needed to get to Tammy and get her to give me that money back. I knew that shit wasn't gonna be easy but I didn't have a choice. I had to come up with a plan.

I sat on my bed feeling bad for Scooter and that I couldn't protect him. He'd been my nigga for most of my life and, because of me being distracted by wanting to get Tammy back, he'd lost his life. That shit made me mad. If Sheila and Tyrone's asses hadn't come into my house, I wouldn't have gotten locked up and Tammy wouldn't have run off with my money. She was gonna give it back to me. All of it. *And* she was gonna come home and stop with that bullshit she called a marriage.

*****

I staked out Sheila's house all day. When I saw Tyrone leave with some big yellow nigga, I took my chance. Getting out the car, I walked up to the door with my gun behind my back. I rang the doorbell and stood out of the view of the peephole. When Tammy opened the door, I pointed the gun at her face.

"I told you I could touch you," I said, smirking.

She backed into the house, her hands up in the air. I saw Sheila sitting on the couch when we walked into the living room. She reached for her phone.

"You wanna be stupid, try me!" I said, taking the gun from Tammy's back and pointing it at Sheila.

She put her phone down and stared at me in disbelief. She looked sick. Like she was knocking at death's door. These bitches just didn't get it. I was desperate. My life hung in the balance of me getting this money from Tammy. She *had* to give it to me. Tammy walked over and sat beside Sheila, both of them seeming to be wait for me to speak.

"Look man, where's the money you took from me. I know you got it," I said, waving the gun frantically.

"I... I don't have it here, Tre," Tammy stammered.

"Well, where the hell is it? And don't drag your fuckin' feet 'cause I know your so-called husband will be back soon."

"It's at my house, Tre. I can take you to it. Just... let's go," she said, getting up.

"Sit down! How I know you ain't setting me up?" I asked, feeling spit in the corners of my mouth.

"Setting you up? Really, Tremaine? Where do I have the time to set you up? You just bust in here, waving a gun, and demanding that I give you that money back and I'm telling you that I have it and yo' paranoid ass is accusing me of plotting against you?" she looked at me like I was crazy.

"How do I know you still have the money?" I asked, not believing her.

"Because my husband said he didn't want your money. He told me that he refused to build anything for us with money that I stole from you. So it's still there in the duffel bag that I took it out of the apartment in. So, let me just give it back to you and you can be on your way," she said like it was that simple.

"Be on my way?" I laughed. "You think I'm gone let you go? Really? You comin' wit' me. You thought I was gonna let you and that nigga live happily ever after? Come on," I demanded.

She walked over to me, looking back at Sheila. I knew that she was gonna call Tyrone as soon as we left. I had to be smart. I wanted to give myself some time to get the hell outta dodge before the dogs came looking for me.

"Gimme your phone," I said to Sheila, holding my hand out.

She got up, looking like she could barely carry her own weight, and handed her phone to me.

"You, too," I said to Tammy.

She reached into her pocket and gave me her phone, too. I pushed my gun into her back and we turned towards the door. Walking out, we got into my car and I made her give me her address. I was gonna make her drive but I didn't wanna leave my car there. This woulda been a time when Scooter would've come in handy. RIP to my nigga, man. You never know what a person means to you until they're gone.

We drove all the way to Old Cloverdale with Tammy looking at me crazy. I wanted to smack the shit out of her but I had other plans for her as soon as I got my money. We pulled up to her house and I instantly got pissed. They were living the life with this nice ass crib and I was living in a fuckin' hotel fuckin ugly bitches for a room.

We walked up to the house and she opened the door. Turning off the alarm, I followed her to the master bedroom. I sat on the bed while she went into the walk-in closet. She came back with my duffel bag. She wasn't lying, it looked like she hadn't touched the money.

"Must be nice to not need a nigga's money. Looks like you upgraded from a trap hoe to an Oprah watchin' housewife," I laughed.

"Tremaine, you got the money, can you please just let me go and gone about your business?" she said with attitude.

Whack! I popped her ass in the mouth, knocking her face down on the bed.

"You uppity all of a sudden? You think you can talk to me any kinda way? I see I need to remind you who the fuck I am," I said, pulling her dress up and ripping her panties off.

I held her down with my body weight and unbuckled my pants, pulling my dick through the hole of my boxers. I shoved myself into her, making her scream.

"Shut the fuck up! All that shit you was talkin' I'm gonna show you how to stay in your place," I yelled, fuckin' her hard.

I pressed her face into the bed to stifle her screams. She was wetter than she'd ever been before. I knew it was because she was pregnant. If I couldn't get her pregnant, I was gonna feed this nigga's baby. I stroked Tammy long and hard, enjoying the feel of her. I hadn't had her in months and I missed the way she fit my dick like a glove, even though she'd been fuckin' Tyrone. Her bottom was further back than I remembered but I refused to accept the fact that he was bigger than me.

I grabbed her around her neck and squatted, digging deeper into her. I rode her ass to ecstasy, squirting as far into her as my dick would go. I let her go and she gasped for air. I could see red marks around her neck where I'd been choking her.

"Get up and clean yo'self up. And put a scarf or some shit 'round yo' neck. It's time to go," I said, smacking her on the ass.

I wasn't gonna give Samson shit. I was taking Tammy and getting on the first plane out of the country. I sat on the bed watching Tammy clean herself up in the bathroom and my dick got hard again. I leaned back on the bed and pulled out a blunt I'd rolled before I left the hotel room. Lighting it, I massaged myself while I watched her, thinking of all the fuckin' I had to make up for.

"Come here."

She walked out of the bathroom slowly, like she was scared of what I was about to do to her. I had the blunt in one hand and the gun in the other.

"Suck my dick," I commanded while I pulled on my blunt.

She got on her knees obediently and wrapped her mouth around my head. I put my gun down and grabbed a handful of her hair. Holding her head steady while I shoved myself all the way down her throat, making her gag and her eyes water. I fucked her mouth, holding her head steady, smoking my blunt and ashing in her hair. The feeling of her throat muscles tightening around me was euphoric. I smoked my blunt to a roach and put it out on the nightstand.

"Don't you dare throw up!" I threatened as I slammed her face against my pelvis, pressing my dick all the way down her throat. "Get up," I yelled.

I was gonna make her pay for leaving me for that fuck nigga Tyrone. I laid her on the bed and pushed her legs back. I was gonna fuck her in her marital bed and make sure I left my seed all over the sheets. Let Tyrone know I was here.

"Say you love me," I said, stroking her long and deep with her legs on my shoulders.

She stared at me with tears streaming down her face but didn't say a word. I wanted to slap her ass. I don't know what had come over her but she was actually being defiant. That nigga had her spoiled. I bet she ran all over his punk ass. I reached back and grabbed my gun.

"Open your mouth," I said, never missing a stroke.

She shook her head 'no'.

"Tammy, don't make me kill you. Open your fuckin' mouth," I said, ramming her hard enough to make her scream out in pain. She was trying to act like she didn't like it but I knew her. I knew she liked that rough shit.

I stuck the gun in her mouth. I knew she wasn't gonna be able to talk now but I didn't care. I was getting off from the fear in her eyes. Knowing that her life was in my hands had me ready to bust but I wanted to make sure I did some real damage to her pussy so she remembered whose it was. I was slick hoping to fuck that baby outta her so I could knock her up with my own.

I was about to cum and didn't want to blow her brains out by mistake. I pulled the gun out of her mouth and, just when I was about to cum, I felt a fist connect with my temple. Before I could turn around and see what was happening, I was dragged by my feet off the bed, my head catching the rail on the way down.

"Fucckkkkk!" I screamed out before I caught another jab in the mouth. I opened my eyes just as Tyrone grabbed me by my throat and stood up lifting me off the ground.

"You kidnap and rape my wife! You in my house in my motherfuckin' bed with a gun in her mouth. You fuckin' coward!"

I felt like my eyes were bulging out of my head and I couldn't breathe. I knew he was about to kill me. At least I'd gotten some ass before I died. I felt myself passing out until I heard Tammy yell.

"Ty! Let him go! Bay, you'll go back to jail!"

I felt my body drop to the floor before I completely lost consciousness.

Tyrone

"Hello," I answered, wondering why Nel was calling me from her office phone.

"Ty! You gotta get over here. Tre came and took Tammy. He came in here with a gun and demanding the money Tammy took out the apartment. I think she took him to your house to get the money but he was talkin' like he's tryna take her with him wherever he's headed," she screamed hoarsely into the phone.

I slammed on the brakes, almost giving Ron whiplash and made an illegal U-turn. If the cops got behind me, they were just gonna have to follow me to my house. I had to get to my wife. There was no tellin' what Tre was doin' to her.

"What's up, man?" Ron asked, looking at me like I was crazy.

"Nel said Tre came to her house with a gun and took Tammy. Said they're headed to my house. Call the cops and a coroner 'cause if I catch this nigga, he dead," I explained.

"Word," Ron said, dialing 911. "Hello. Yes, I'd like to report a kidnapping. My sister-in-law was taken at gunpoint from my fiancée's house. She said he was headed to my brother-in-law's house. The address... what's your address, Ty?" he turned to me.

"433 Thorn Place," I said, my eyes fixed on the road.

I was focused. I knew every second I wasn't there was another second that Tre could kill Tammy. He was the type that would kill her before letting anybody else have her and I knew my baby wasn't gonna just lay down and let him take her and our son away from me. That meant he was even more likely to hurt her to try and turn her back into that broken, damaged woman that he knew.

We pulled up in my driveway and there was a black Toyota Celica in the driveway. I figured it was Tre's car. Ron was on the phone with Nel trying to calm her down. I didn't have time to waste so I left his ass in the car and got out, headed to the house. I heard a scream that sounded like it came from our bedroom. I felt my ears start to ring. I walked to the window and looked in. I saw Tre on top of my wife with a gun in her mouth. I knew that I couldn't risk startling him or he might fuck around and shoot her.

Walking back around to the front door, I bumped into Ron. He was off the phone with Sheila and had his nine drawn. I walked in with him right behind me, hoping the chime didn't let Tre know I was coming in the house. When I didn't hear the chirp, I smiled.

That's my girl, I thought knowing Tammy had silenced the chime.

My baby knew I was coming for her. We crept through the house to the bedroom and it took everything in me not to hit that nigga as soon as I got to the door. I had to stand there, watching while he raped my wife, until he took the gun out of her mouth. As soon as he did though, I took my opportunity.

I walked over and caught him with a right hook that knocked him off Tammy. I grabbed him by his ankles and pulled his ass off the bed. He hit his head on the rail and let out a scream. I didn't care. He was gonna feel my wrath. I jabbed him in the mouth before standing up with his ass, my hands wrapped around his throat. I was about to kill him. I watched the life leaving his body as his body dangled. He was a few inches shorter than me, but that didn't matter because I had his ass up as far as my arms would let me lift him.

I'd blacked out. I felt Ron's arms on mine, trying to get me to let go but that shit wasn't fazing me. Then I heard Tammy's voice.

"Ty! Let him go! Bay, you'll go back to jail!"

I snapped out of it and dropped him. He passed out on the floor and I heard knocks on my front door. I knew it was the cops. Ron went to answer the door. I walked over Tre's body and took my wife into my arms. I was holding her as she cried into my shoulder when the police came in. I looked up and saw that it was the same Officers from the vandalism case and the hospital last night.

"Y'all might as well move in," I said sarcastically.

"I was saying the same thing when we got the call, Mr. Price," Officer Taylor laughed.

"Does the entire city of Montgomery have it out for y'all?" Officer Smith asked, shaking his head and looking down at Tre.

"He's working with Delilah," I explained. "This is my wife's ex. I guarantee him coming over here has something to do with Delilah and probably Samson, too."

I didn't mention the money because Ron had already put it back in the closet before going to answer the door. That dude was on-point. We were gonna get along just fine. He wasn't even all the way up-to-date with what was goin' on but he took precautions. Let me know he was streetwise as hell.

"Mrs. Price, do you need an ambulance?" Officer Taylor asked Tammy.

She looked up from my shoulder and nodded. Officer Taylor walked away and radioed for an ambulance.

"Mr. Price, can you come give me a statement?" Officer Smith asked.

I didn't want to leave Tammy but I knew that this had to be done. I didn't like the fact that cops knew me by name and all this shit had happened to us, in new our house, in less than a year of us moving in. I was sure the neighbors were wondering what the hell kinda shit we were involved in that warranted regular visits by the cops. I was waiting on the letter from the Neighborhood Association.

"So, what happened here?" Officer Smith asked me, taking his notebook out of his front pocket and sitting down at the dining room table. Officer Taylor was getting Tammy's statement.

"I got a call from my sister telling me that Tre..."

"The man passed out on the floor," he interrupted me for clarity.

"Yeah. She told me that he'd come to her house and taken my wife by gunpoint. Said he thought she'd taken some money from their apartment when he'd got locked up for shooting her a few months ago. My sister is battling cancer so I know Tammy coaxed him out of her house over here to save her life," I explained.

"Did she take the money he was talking about?" he asked skeptically.

"NO. We both work hard. Everything we have we earned. I don't know what the hell he's talking about," I lied.

"So why bring him here?" he asked like I hadn't told him that already.

"To get him away from my sister, I just told you she's sick and because she knew I would be here as soon as my sister called me. Search him. I bet he got both their phones. My sister called me from her home office phone," I explained, watching as the paramedics came to tend to Tammy. I knew my wife was a fighter but I hoped our son was ok.

"Ok, Mr. Price. And what happened when you got here?"

"He was on top of my wife raping her with his gun in her mouth. I came in, Tammy had turned off the chime, and I walked in the room. I had to wait 'til he moved the gun from her mouth so I had to stand there and watch him rapin' her. As soon as he moved that gun, I whooped his ass. Tammy saved his life 'cause I was about to choke the life out the nigga," I admitted.

"Well, we're both glad you didn't do that," he said, shaking his head. The look on his face said he would have done the same thing.

"Now what?" I asked.

"Your wife is going to have a rape kit done. We've dispatched an officer to your sister's house so that we can get her statement. And we're gonna take your intruder downtown with us," he said, getting up from his seat.

"Have y'all found Delilah?" I asked.

"We were headed to the address you gave us last night when we got the call to come here. So no, we haven't found her yet."

"Offer that nigga a deal and I bet he deliver her and Samson to y'all. Samson is wanted for the assault on my mother, right?" I asked, making sure there was a warrant for both of their asses.

"Yes sir. And we'll look into getting information from him when we get to the station. I hope you and your wife can get some peace soon," he said sincerely.

"Me, too," I said walking back into the bedroom to check on Tammy.

"How you doin', bay?" I asked her as she laid on the gurney ready to be transported.

"I'm as ok as can be expected," she forced a smile.

"Where y'all takin' her?" I asked.

"She requested to go to the rape crisis center. It's in the One Place Family Justice Center building on South Lawrence Street. Here's their card," the medic offered, giving me the card.

"I'll be right behind you, ok," I promised Tammy.

"Y'all go check on Nel. I'll be ok. Come after you done took Ron to his wife to be."

"Bay..." I started to protest.

"Gone now, Tyrone. I want to do this alone, please. Just meet me at the hospital. They're gonna check on the baby after I leave the other place," she said, not taking no for an answer.

I wanted to be there with her every step of the way but I had to respect her wishes. I watched, trying not to cry, as they wheeled my wife out of the house. Tre was coming to. They wasted no time cuffing his ass. I swear I wanted to lay hands on his ass again. When they'd led him to their car and left and everyone was gone from our house, I locked up and took Ron to Nel's house.

My mind was consumed with thoughts of Tammy but I waited until they called me and told me that she was at the hospital. I rushed to her side. She said our son was ok, but I still wanted to be there for her. I never wanted to leave her side again. I was starting to think like Ron and wanting to get my family the hell outta this city. I'd run it by Tammy when I got to the hospital.

Beth

When Samantha and I got back from New Orleans, we parted ways, agreeing to meet up at the Renaissance. Just because we were hiding out didn't mean our vacation had to end early. I went to my parents' to pack more clothes. We figured the cops would catch Delilah's ass in the next week or so and then we could go on with our lives. Anthony had told Sam that he was gonna take the kids to the Embassy Suites and tell them that it was a mini-vacation, so we'd chosen the Renaissance, too, so we could be close to them.

I'd checked in and was in the room, getting ready to go get in the pool and I hadn't heard anything from Sam. I was starting to get worried. It wasn't like her to not let me know that she was at least ok. My mind started to race. I didn't wanna be paranoid but I had a bad gut feeling. I grabbed my phone.

"Hey Anthony. Is Samantha there with y'all?" I asked, thinking she'd stopped by there before coming to me.

"No, I was waiting to hear from her. She ain't with you?" he asked, sounding concerned.

"She went to the house to pack some stuff and I haven't heard anything from her since," I said, scared. "I think I need to go over there and make sure she's ok."

"Did you call her?"

"Of course I called her," I said, sounding insulted.

"I was just checking. You know how you women overreact and sometimes forget to do the simple shit," he laughed.

"Fuck you! Now's not the time for your shit."

"Don't be mad at me because your estrogen supersedes your logic sometimes."

"Bye, man," I said about to hang up the phone.

"Look Beth," he said, catching me before I hit the end button. "My girl is a cop. I'll send her over there. Don't you go anywhere in case something's wrong. We don't need both of y'all to go missing."

"Fine," I said with attitude. "Please let me know what she finds out. And I'll let you know if I hear anything from her."

"Bet," he said, hanging up.

"You have reached Samantha Johnson. I'm sorry I missed your call. But if you leave your name, number, and the reason for your call and I'll get back to you at my earliest convenience," her phone went straight to voicemail. I hadn't been completely honest with Anthony. I hadn't called her. I had gone straight to panicking. But her phone going straight to voicemail added to my panic.

I sat, rocking back and forth, trying to tell myself not to worry. I hoped that Anthony's cop girlfriend would go by and tell us what's going on. I checked my phone... Nothing. I decided to call Delilah to make sure she wasn't on some dumb shit.

"Well, well, well..." she answered the phone with a laugh.

"Delilah, where are you?" I asked, frustrated.

"You're not worried about where I am. You're lookin' for your lil' girlfriend," she said, confirming my fears.

"Delilah..."

"If she gives us what we want, she'll live to eat your pussy another day."

She hung up the phone in my face. I didn't know what to do so I called Anthony back.

"Beth, I haven't heard anything yet. Chill the fuck out... Sarabi, put that down and get off your brother's back! Have you lost your mind?!" I heard him scream at the children.

"Delilah's got Sam," I told him.

"What you mean she's *got Sam*?"

"Just what I said. I called her phone and she told me that Sam needs to give them what they want and she'd live."

"They? Who is they?"

"I assume it's her and Samson. Or maybe it's her, Tre, and Scooter. I don't fuckin' know," I said, getting flustered.

"Ok, I'll call you right back. I'm gonna call Keisha and see what she's found out."

"Keisha?" I asked, not knowing who he was talking about.

"Yeah, Keisha. Look, I don't have time to spell this shit out for you. I gotta find my wife."

He hung up the phone. I was about tired of people hanging up the phone on me. I decided to do something. I figured they were at Sam's house so I decided to go to my apartment. I had to help Sam. I grabbed my purse, checking to make sure my gun was in there. I planned to shoot first and ask questions later when the time came.

Delilah

I sat in Samantha's house waiting for her to come in. I'd been here since Anthony left with his little girlfriend because I needed a place to hide out. I knew it would only be a matter of time until they came looking for me at Beth's house. Samson was somewhere taking care of Scooter and Tre. He told me to call him once I had Samantha. The way he saw it, the money that she had was his. Her momma didn't spend it like he'd told her to so he wanted the money back, with interest. I didn't care. The more time he spent doing other shit, including whatever he was about to do to Samantha, the less time he spent fucking with me.

I heard keys in the door. I sat still, gun pointed at the entrance in case it wasn't Sam. When she turned on the lights, I wasted no time. I stood up and shot her in the right knee.

"*Aaah!*" she screamed, falling to the floor.

I had to admit I was getting a rush from all the damage I was doin' to these weak motherfuckers. It reminded me of watching Daniella burning up in the house while the police questioned me. Hearing her scream until she was burned to a crisp. Watching the entire structure collapse while the Firefighters tried to get the fire under control.

"I figured you'd put up a fight so I decided to go ahead and nip that shit in the bud. I don't feel like wrestlin' with no damn body else," I said, walking up and standing over her.

"Delilah, what the fuck you doin' in my house?" she asked, grabbing at her leg.

"You didn't think it was a good idea to change your fuckin' code after you fired me? I mean, really Sam, I thought you were smarter than that," I laughed looking at her pitiful ass.

"Man, what you want?" she asked, looking at me like she wanted to kill me.

"Samson wants the money your momma gave you. You know what, I'll let him explain the shit to you. Get up," I ordered her, ready to get this shit over with.

"Get up? How you expect me to walk when you just shot me in the got damn knee you crazy bitch," she yelled.

"You better figure it out. Crawl if you got to. But hurry the fuck up," I said, walking towards the door.

I saw her reach for in her pocket and pull out her phone. I shot again, making it explode in her hand.

"Why the fuck do they keep trying me?" I said aloud, stomping over and dragging Samantha's ass up and helping her out the door.

I threw her ass in the backseat of my car so she didn't try anything. I figured the cops had been to Beth's house and were gone by now since they couldn't find me. I was headed there. On the way, I called Samson.

"Hey, I got Samantha," I said into the phone.

"Ok. Are you headed back to the apartment? I watched the cops and they came and went. They won't be back there lookin' for us anytime soon," he said what I'd just thought aloud. It was scary how he was in my head.

"Yeah. And it's late so the property manager should be gone and the nosy ass neighbors won't be watching. I can drag Samantha's ass on in the house and we'll be waiting on you."

"Drag her in? Why would you have to drag her in?" Samson asked, his voice showing his irritation.

"Yeah, I had to shoot her. Just in her knee, though, so she can still walk," I explained, feeling like a child in trouble.

"What the fuck is your problem, Delilah? You stab Tanisha and now you shoot Sam. How is she gonna go in the bank and get the money now? They're gonna notice that she's been shot," he yelled into the phone.

"She can't just get it from the ATM or the drive thru?" I asked, frustrated.

"Yeah, they're gonna give her two hundred fifty thousand dollars at an ATM or drive-thru teller. Are you stupid or really just that fuckin' crazy?" he yelled, hanging up the phone before I could answer.

"Uggghhhh!" Samantha groaned from the back seat.

"Shut the fuck up," I yelled, turning around to look at her, making me swerve.

I sped all the way back to Beth's apartment. I knew Samson was gonna punish me for shooting Samantha's ass. I really hadn't thought that one through. Oh well, she deserved to be shot. That bitch wasn't innocent by anyone's account. I was gonna be the hand of karma on all these motherfuckers.

I parked and got out, going to open the door before I went back to drag Sam's crippled ass in the house. I was surprised they hadn't changed the locks. But I would've just broken in if they had so it didn't matter. I walked in and looked around. Nothing looked out of place but something felt off. I couldn't put my finger on it so I just shrugged it off as paranoia and went to get Sam before her whining woke up the neighbors. It was times like this I wished Beth's ass had a house. I would have more privacy. But I had to deal with what I had. Walking back over to the car, I pointed the gun at Sam's head.

"You betta not make a single fuckin' sound, you hear me. Not a peep, or your kids will be going to your funeral, understood," I threatened.

She nodded her head that she understood and I pulled her out of the car and helped her limp to the door. When we got in the house, I pushed her down on the couch and sat waiting for Samson to get back. When he walked through the door, I felt like I was about to piss myself. I didn't know what was about to happen.

He walked in and assessed the situation. Sam lay on the couch, holding her leg, dried blood all down the leg of her jeans. Samson walked over and sat down beside her.

"Hi Samantha. Do you know who I am?" he asked, smiling at her.

"Yeah," she said grimacing.

"God you look just like your momma," he said, wiping the sweat from her forehead.

I felt myself getting jealous. He never handled me that gently. I wanted to get up and shoot her in the face and him in the head. He must have felt me staring at them because he turned to me with fire in his eyes.

"Go get some fuckin' towels and pain meds. I know your little girlfriend got something in here that'll help her with the pain. She coulda bled to death," he snapped at me.

I got up, looking at him with a look that could kill.

"Leave that fuckin' gun on the table. I don't like the way you lookin' at me," he said and I obeyed. He must have sensed that I planned to shoot his ass in the back of the head. That's ok, my chance would present itself I'm sure.

I walked into the bathroom and grabbed some towels and searched the medicine cabinet until I found some Vicodin. I popped one before I walked out of the bathroom. I felt pain coming my way from Samson after he finished tending to his dear Samantha. I took him the towels and pills and watched as he treated Samantha like she was precious cargo. Made me happy I'd shot her ass. When he'd propped her up on the couch and turned on the TV to make sure she was comfortable, he turned to me.

I thought he was gonna fuss or tell me to come in the back with him. Instead, he grabbed a handful of my extensions and dragged me down the hallway. I tried to fight him but it was no use. I was glad that I'd taken that Vicodin because those carpet burns were gonna hurt like fuck in the morning. He threw me up against the bed and started to unbuckle his pants. I prepared myself for the sexual assault but he took his belt off and wrapped it around my neck. Tightening it by feeding the leather through the buckle, he pulled me up off of the ground by it.

"I should murder you for what you did to my daughter," he spat in my ear.

Unable to speak, I looked at him in disbelief. I was his daughter, too. Why didn't he see that? He choked me until I damn hear passed out, looking at me like I didn't deserve to live.

"You don't even deserve my dick," he said when he finally let me go. "You're weak like your fuckin' daddy and twice as crazy as your hoe ass momma," he said, walking away.

I couldn't believe my ears. Was he saying that he wasn't my father? Who was my father, then? I lay there, trying to catch my breath and make sense of what I'd just heard. I couldn't stop myself from crying. I cried until I had no more tears. I thought of ending my life but decided to take Samson's instead. And that of his pride and joy, his biological daughter, Samantha. But not before I got some got damned answers.

Anthony

"I'm kinda busy right now, Kris. This better be important, you've called me six times back-to-back. What is it?" Keisha said when she finally answered her phone.

"My wife... Samantha is missing," I said into the phone, quietly so the children didn't hear.

"I'm in the middle of an investigation and you called me about your *wife*? You've got to be fuckin' kiddin' me. Look, I'll call you when I get off. I'm trying to find a psychopath so playing hide and go seek with your wife isn't necessarily a priority for me right now," she said, hanging up the phone.

I wanted to be upset but I understood where Keisha was coming from. She was working and here I was calling her about my wife who was known for her disappearing acts. I used to tell Sam about that shit. I told her we'd never know if something really happened to her ass until it was too late because of the way her ass got ghost when things weren't goin' her way. But this time felt different. I knew something was wrong. Especially seeing that she didn't take Beth with her wherever she went. I called Beth to see if she'd heard from Sam.

"Hey you've reached Beth. You know what to do at the beep!" The call went straight to voicemail.

Now I couldn't get either of them on the phone. I decided not to worry myself about Sam and her girlfriend. For all I knew, they could have been fuckin' and that's why they weren't answering the phone. I focused on my kids, getting them ready for bed. When they were all tucked in, I went out onto the balcony to smoke a Newport. I had to calm my nerves. As badly as I didn't want to worry about Sam, I couldn't shake the feeling that she wasn't ok.

I finished my square and walked back into the hotel room and picked up the envelope that held the divorce papers I'd had drawn up before I went and got the kids from my mom's. As ready as I was to get this over with so that Keisha and I could be together for real, I still had my concerns. I still loved Sam, I just wasn't in love with her. I don't think I ever was. I didn't realize that until I met Keisha. With Keisha, it was different. I could see being with her and only her for the rest of my life. And I wanted to tell her just that.

Pushing the thoughts of Sam from my mind, I sat, waiting for Keisha to call me when she got off. Even though she said we needed a break, I knew that was just her way of telling me that she wanted to see if I was serious about her. At ten o'clock, just like clockwork, my phone rang Miguel's *Coffee*. I picked it up and stepped back out onto the balcony.

"Hey beautiful," I smiled into the phone.

"Hello Kris," she said, sounding agitated.

"Everything ok?" I asked.

"No. Where are you?" she asked.

"At the Embassy Suites. I've got my kids with me, though. So you'd have to come up to the room and join me on the balcony if you want to see me."

I hoped that she was asking me where I was so she could come see me. Sex may have been hard on the inside with the kids in the room, but we could get creative on the balcony.

"What room? I'll grab us a six pack and come chill with you. I've had a long, crazy ass day and you're the closest thing to sane I have," she said.

"Room 425," I offered eagerly.

"Ok. See you in about an hour."

I jumped up and ran to the shower. I needed to freshen up after a day of playing monster and swimming with the little ones. I was excited to see Keisha and the fact that she wanted to see me after she'd had a long day spoke volumes.

After I freshened up, I checked the children to make sure they were asleep. They were knocked out. I went back to the balcony to smoke another cigarette when there was a light knock on the door.

I walked over and opened it to find Keisha in sweats with a six-pack of Budweiser in hand.

"Come on in," I stepped back so she could come into the room.

"Oh my goodness, they're adorable!" she gushed looking at my children.

"Yeah, I've got pretty good genes."

"More like their momma got good genes because they don't look like you. None but the little one," she said pointing to Sarabi.

"That's my little shadow there," I smiled looking at my baby girl. "Come on, let's sit on the balcony."

We went out and enjoyed the night air. At first neither of us said anything, we just drank our beer and looked out over the city.

"I filed for divorce," I broke the silence. "I really like you and want to do this the right way. I want you to be my forever."

"Wow, that's a bomb to drop," she blushed. "You did that for me? What if we don't work out?"

"Regardless of whether we work out or not, Sam and I don't need to be together. We got married because she got pregnant. There's always been love but this was more a situation of convenience than one of real feelings for each other. She didn't want to be alone and I was comfortable."

"And I'm different?" she asked with a raised eyebrow.

"Yeah... yeah, you are. The feelings I have when I'm with you I've never had with Samantha or anyone else. If anyone deserves an honest try from me, you do."

"Well, that's a pleasant turn on my night," she smiled at me.

"So, what's goin' on," I asked, hoping she'd caught Delilah. At least then I'd know the chances of Sam being ok would be better than they would be with Delilah still roaming the streets. Beth had said that Delilah had her but I didn't have any proof of that and wasn't gonna send Keisha on a wild goose chase.

"Well, I'm not really supposed to be discussing this with you seeing that your lot is involved in this whole mess. But I really need another take on it," she said, taking a swig of her beer.

"So, it seems like there's six degrees of separation between you and the other parties involved in three cases I'm working right now. But the common denominator is this Delilah Powell. She vandalized this couple's house. Tyrone Price and his wife, I think you told me he's your business partner?"

"Yeah, he is."

"Well, she shot his and his wife's cars up and threw a brick in the window that had a note attached. The note read, 'no happily ever after'. Then it turns out that she got the car that she was driving during the vandalism from your lot. Last night, I get a call to Jackson Hospital and find out that the patient was stabbed by Delilah and that she's Tyrone and your ex, Sheila's, mom. Then today, I get a call about a kidnapping and a rape. Apparently, Sheila's son's father came into her house and held her and Tyrone's wife, Tammy, at gunpoint before kidnapping Tammy and taking her back to her house looking for money he claims she stole from him when he was locked up. I guess he didn't get it because he proceeded to rape the woman, even shoving his gun in her mouth. Her husband goes home after his sister calls him and tells him what's goin' on and beats the shit outta dude. It's a wonder he didn't kill him. Hell, I would have. Anyway, we take this man, a Tremaine McDaniels, downtown and he begs us for a deal. Says he can get us Samson, the man responsible for beating Sheila's mom up before Delilah stabbed her, and that Samson could lead us to Delilah. Right now, we're waiting to see what the DA wants to do about the situation," she said, guzzling the rest of her beer.

"Damn baby," I said. My head was spinning just from hearing the summary of the shit she was dealing with. But more than that, my head was spinning because I didn't realize Delilah was that damn crazy.

My mind drifted back to Sam and wondered if she was ok. I knew she and Delilah were sisters so that meant that Samson was her father, too. He may have come after her and her money. I decided not to bring this up, though. Not until I knew something was really wrong with Sam.

"That's all I get? Damn baby?"

"I'm just floored. I didn't know Delilah was unstable like that."

"Makes you wanna be more careful where you stick your dick, huh?" she said, smirking.

"Yeah, it does," I smiled at her slick ass remark. "You're throwin' shade as my kids say."

"Damn you sound like an old man. You better be happy your kids are cute or I'd have to give you the axe. I don't play step-momma."

"Oh no?" I asked pulling her up and into my lap. "How about momma? You want kids?"

"You got enough for the both of us," she laughed. "I like my body nice and tight just like it is, thank you very much."

We kissed for a while before she stood up and took off her sweatpants. Pulling my dick out, I leaned back in the chair while she straddled me and rode my dick. All of my thoughts of Samantha melted away. I stroked her worries about work away, too. We drank and talked and made love until the sun came up. She left before the kids got up and I got in the bed with Kwame and tried to sleep off my buzz before they got up asking for breakfast.

Sheila

I was tired. I'd had enough of Delilah and Tre and all of 'em and was ready to get Jeff and run away with Ron, leaving this fuckin' city behind. I knew it wasn't gonna be easy to leave everything I knew, but I was gonna do it so I could have a fresh start and an honest chance at love. I'd called my doctor and they told me that they would transfer my information to the Winship Cancer Institute of Emory University when I moved. I was moving slowly getting dressed for my meeting with the executives of Vantech. As weak as I was, I had a full day ahead of me. After that meeting, I was gonna go see Tanisha in the hospital. As much of a risk as it was, I needed to see her and make sure she was ok. She was my mother, after all. Then, Ron, Shawn, and I were meeting everyone at the Mojo Lounge building so that we could go over the particulars of the Grand Opening. Everyone in one place was gonna be interesting. I picked up my phone and made a call.

"Hello? Anthony?" I said once he answered the phone. I heard his children in the background. I was happy he was spending time with them.

"Sheila? Hi! How are you?" he asked sounding happy to hear my voice. I couldn't understand why I got butterflies.

"I'm well, thank you. Look, I wanted to make sure you and Samantha were still gonna be able to meet me at the Lounge this afternoon at three. We're all meeting there to go over everything for the Grand Opening," I said, keeping it as professional as possible.

"I'll be there. Sam, I'm not so sure about. She's pulled one of her disappearing acts," he said.

"Is she ok?" I asked, immediately thinking about Delilah and all the other foolishness that I'd been dealing with.

"I hope so. I haven't heard from her in a couple days and now her girlfriend's missing, too."

Girlfriend? Did I hear that right? What the hell did they have goin' on? I thought to myself but then dismissed it because it wasn't any of my business. *Not my circus, not my monkeys.*

"Ok. Well, I was about to call her next, so I hope she can attend the meeting. I won't be here too much longer so I want to make sure that things are to y'alls satisfaction," I said.

"Won't be here? You ok?"

"Yeah. Jeff and I are moving with my fiancé to Atlanta. He got a job with Jive Records and asked me to come with him," I beamed.

"Oh," he said, dryly.

"Well, I'll see you this afternoon," I said, wanting to end the call before the conversation went left. I hadn't talked to him since I left his ass sitting at The Egg & I, and I didn't want to be pulled into his web again.

"Sheil..." I ended the call before he could even get my name out of his mouth. I really wasn't in the mood for any mind games right now.

I looked through my contacts and found Samantha's number. I called and it went straight to voicemail. I decided to leave a message.

"Hi Samantha. This is Sheila Price. I was calling to remind you about the meeting that we scheduled a couple of weeks ago at the Mojo Lounge building at three this afternoon. I want to go over some important details and need all parties involved present. Please give me a call or shoot me a text to confirm. Hope all is well."

I buttoned up my shirt and tucked it into my slacks. I wasn't in a power suit kinda mood. I really wanted this day to be over with already. I dragged my feet walking into the kitchen to get my coffee and Ron was sitting at the table. He scared the shit outta me.

"Hey Bae! I thought you went home to get some clothes and get dressed for today."

"Ummmm, I *am* dressed for today. And I did go home. You ok? I been gone for hours," he asked, his brow furrowed.

"Yeah, I'm good. I guess. I'm still fucked up about Tanisha and what Tre did to Tammy. I feel like I should have done something, ya know," I said, pouring coffee into my tumbler.

"Look, you know Shawn and I can handle everything after the executive meeting today so you can rest. You're still recovering from your chemo. I don't know why your stubborn ass won't reschedule so you can regain your strength."

"The world don't wait for you to regain your strength, bae. The reason I'm who I am and in the position I'm in is because I know what has to be done and don't let anything prevent me from making it happen."

"This ain't anything, Nel. This is your *health* we're talkin' about. Look, I ain't 'bout to argue with you. You ready to go?" he asked, getting up from the table and walking to the door.

"Ron, don't be like that. I get it, you're worried about me. I love you for it. But this needs to be done. I wanna tie up all these loose ends so there's nothing for me to do but pack up and move to the A with my soon-to-be husband," I said making him blush. I walked over and stood on my tiptoes and kissed him passionately.

"Alright, keep on and you gone be late for your meeting. Kissin' me like I won't lay yo' ass 'cross that table and have yo' ass for breakfast," he said and I winked at him.

"We'll have plenty of time for that later. I'll make sure to save enough energy for that."

I walked past him twitching my ass out the door. I loved this man. Like I never loved anybody before. He was just.... different. And I liked his different. The fact that Jeff loved him was just the icing on the cake. They played video games and went out together. He was a great father to my son. Speaking of... I needed to make sure I was still able to have kids because I definitely wanted to give him one. I made a mental note to ask my doctor about that when Ron wasn't around.

We got in the car and he blasted Big KRIT all the way to the office. I vibed and got ready for this meeting. I had no idea how things were gonna go but I was ready for whatever.

"Her pussy tighter than pliers and squeeze the wine outta grapes," Ron rapped along with KRIT, grabbing my thigh.

I blushed and looked at him with lust in my eyes. I was having all kinds of impure thoughts about this man on my way to work. I had to look out the window and distract myself with the scenery to keep from reaching into his jeans and giving the cars passing us a show. I'd been watchin' Auntie Angel videos so I was more than ready to try out my new head techniques.

We pulled up to Vantech and my face was flushed. I had to get my head back in the game. I walked into the building and straight to my office with Ron on my heels.

"Sheila! How you feeling?" Shawn asked giving me a tight hug. He had no idea that I was gonna recommend him for a promotion today.

"I'm good, doll. Ready to get this meeting over. But I've got a burst of energy from somewhere," I looked back at Ron blushing. He was dapping Shawn up and Shawn laughed, giving a knowing look.

"The meeting starts in an hour. You need anything in the meantime?"

"No Hun, but thank you so much... for everything," I said walking into my office. "I'll see you in a lil' bit. Ron and I are gonna go over some things to get me ready for this meeting and the one this afternoon. Have you heard from Samantha? She's the only person who hasn't confirmed. Well, aside from Delilah but with the cops lookin' for that ass, I didn't expect to see her anyway," I said, laughing and shaking my head.

"Naw, I haven't, but I'll call her again and let you know if I hear anything back," Shawn picked up his phone to call Samantha for me.

"Thanks, Shawn. Page me if anyone needs me before it's time for the meeting, ok?"

"I gotcha," he said, smiling at me and Ron. He knew what was up.

The door wasn't closed behind us good before Ron walked up behind me with his mouth on my ear.

"Let me take the edge off before your meeting," he whispered unbuttoning my shirt.

I arched my back into him and enjoyed the feeling of him grabbing a handful of my breasts. I moaned softly as he tweaked my nipples. I turned and looked him in the eyes. I got butterflies in my belly at the sight of him. He kissed me, his tongue telling me he meant business before trailing his kisses down my neck and ravaging my breasts. I missed him so much I felt like I was gonna spontaneously combust. My insides were hot and it felt like I had a waterfall between my legs. He took his time, not even touching my pants. I reached for his and he pushed my hands away. I laid back on my desk while he sucked on my nipples until they were so erect they almost hurt. The warmth of his mouth against my hardened flesh had me wanting to scream.

Since he wouldn't let me handle his manhood, I grabbed two handfuls of his locs. Finally, he unbuttoned and unzipped my pants, they fell around my ankles and I kicked off my shoes so I could free myself. He reached down and massaged me through my lace boy shorts. Feeling how wet I was, he looked at me with a grin on his face. I knew it was gonna take every bit of self-control not to holler so loud they heard me at reception. Squatting down, he kissed my thighs, lifting me up and placing me on the desk. He nibbled and sucked on my clit, never removing my panties. I sighed, getting frustrated. I wanted him and he was playing.

"Ron," I said through clenched teeth.

"Shhhh," he said, moving my panties to the side and sticking his tongue deep inside of me.

"Mmmmm," I moaned, using his locs to hold his head steady as he alternated between tongue-fucking me and sucking on my clit.

I shook and came all over his face and he drank every drop of me up. I was ready to feel him but he stood up and smiled at me. I knew I was gonna have to wait for that. I was upset but I was happy too, because I wouldn't have been able to control myself if he gave me the dick right now.

He frowned as he tried to push his noticeable erection down in his pants. He was going into the meeting with me and that wouldn't have been a good look. I laughed to myself at the thought of it.

"I'm glad my pain is funny to you," he said cutting his eyes at me but smiling.

"You the one playin'. You know I hate getting head without gettin' fucked. I mean, who does that? You lit the fuse. Come on and Blowitup," I said, playing on his nickname.

"That was lame as fuck, Nel," he said, laughing. "Thank you though, 'cause you just killed that hard-on I had."

I laughed with him.

"Miss Price," Shawn came over the intercom.

"Yeah, Shawn," I pushed the button and answered.

"They're ready," he said.

"Ok. I'll be out shortly," I said before sliding off my desk and collecting my pants and shoes.

I pulled my pants on, buttoning my top and tucking it in. I put on my shoes, looked at my reflection in the mirror and took a deep breath.

"You ready?" Ron asked sensing my tension.

"As ready as I'll ever be," I said, opening the door and walking out.

I walked to the conference room with Ron on my left and Shawn on my right. I felt like I was ready to take over the world with these two at my side. Walking in, the other four executives, Mr. Tabb, Mr. Sheldon, Mr. Huffman, and Mr. Abernathy, all stood and greeted me. I went around shaking hands before taking my seat. Ron and Shawn sat in the chairs along the wall. I wasted no time getting to business.

"I requested this meeting for several reasons. I love being a part of the Vantech family. And I know that we have discussed expanding to other cities with larger markets. I want to propose an expansion into Atlanta, Georgia and I feel that it would be especially beneficial to do so with the Urban Division. Shawn," I motioned for him to bring the folders.

As he laid the folders in front of the gentlemen, I continued, "The 2016 Neilson Report considers the African-American population voracious media consumers, powerful cultural influencers experiencing burgeoning population growth that will create an unprecedented impact across a broad range of industries, particularly in television, music, social media, and social issues, as you'll see in the article that is at the front of your proposal packets there. Fifty-four percent of the Atlanta population is African-American and I feel that it would be a smart move for us to branch out and tap into that market."

"Interesting. We'd discussed this before and you weren't really enthusiastic about moving. Why the change of heart now?" Mr. Abernathy, the CEO of the company, asked.

"Well, honestly, my reasoning is both professional and personal. I want to see Vantech win and feel that, though we are leading the market here, we're doing ourselves an injustice by not expanding. And, personally," I said, looking at Ron and smiling, "I have recently become engaged and my fiancé is moving to the Atlanta area for a career opportunity. I'm going with him but don't want to sever ties with Vantech to do so. I'm hoping that you share my desire to keep me as a part of the company."

"Well, congratulations are in order!" Mr. Abernathy said coming over and hugging me. "When do we meet the lucky fellow?"

"Right now," I said looking at Ron again. He got up and walked over to stand beside me. "Gentlemen, this is my fiancé Ronald Roberts," I beamed.

"Nice to meet you," he said, walking around and shaking everyone's hand.

"So, you're taking our Sheila away from us, huh? You must be one hell of a guy because she's the most business-oriented person I know," Mr. Tabb, the President and my mentor, said.

"Yes, sir," Ron said looking down at me proudly.

"Well, I think this is something that we can definitely consider," Mr. Abernathy said, looking at the other Executives who nodded in agreement. "We'll review your packet and get back to you in the next day or so," he smiled.

I knew that meant it was already done. They started to close their folders and get ready to leave.

"Before we adjourn, there's one more thing," I said, looking up at Ron and he nodded, urging me to go ahead.

"Since I will be leaving, I would like to recommend Shawn Graham as my replacement here. He's shown his knowledge of the business and knows the inner workings of Vantech, probably better than some of us," I said, smiling at Shawn whose mouth was wide open. "I have the utmost faith in his abilities and he has a rapport with all of my promoters and business owners in the area. He has been handling things for me with my illness and I think he'd serve us well managing the Montgomery Urban Marketing Division... *if* we decide to expand, that is."

Mr. Tabb let out a laugh. I knew he was proud of me. He'd taught me everything I knew, including being loyal to those who were loyal to you. And Shawn had been beyond loyal.

"I think he'd be ideal for the position, *if* we expand, that is," Mr. Tabb smiled broadly.

"Well gentlemen, that's all I have for you. I'll let you return to your business for the day and look forward to hearing your decision."

They rose and left. Ron kissed me on the forehead, "Great job, baby."

Shawn sat frozen in his seat, still in shock.

"Boy, pick your jaw up off the floor. I told you when I hired you that I knew you were goin' places," I laughed.

"Sheila thank you so much," he smiled from ear-to-ear. "I never woulda thought..."

"What? You thought you were gonna be an executive assistant for the rest of your life? Not on my watch," I said, walking over and hugging him. "I got you. Always," I whispered in his ear as he hugged me tightly.

"Hey. Get off my woman, now," Ron said playing jealous.

Shawn let me go and we walked back to my office. I knew he was about to call his fiancée and tell her the news. I was ready to go see Tanisha for a little while then head back to the house so Ron could finish what he started earlier and I could take a nap before the meeting at three.

"Shawn, I got both my phones so hit me if you need me. Still nothing from Samantha?" I asked, getting concerned.

"Nothing yet," he said, reading the worry on my face. "You think something's wrong?"

"I sure hope not. Look, I'm headed to the hospital to see Tanisha and then to the house to get some rest before this meeting. See you at the Mojo Lounge at three?" I asked.

"Sure will," he said, picking up the phone.

Ron and I left headed to Jackson Hospital.

"Hey bae, I gotta few things to do before we head to the house. I'mma drop you here so you and your mom can get some one-on-one time and I'll be back to scoop you in an hour, ok?" he said, pulling up to the entrance.

"OK," I said, confused wondering what he had to do but didn't question him.

I got out and walked in to check on my mom. I hoped they would be discharging her soon.

Tre

I sat, sweating while they taped the wire to me. I wasn't a snitch but this was the only way I could get the deal and protection I needed. Officer Taylor leaned in front of me, making sure that everything was intact. She was so close I could smell her perfume. She smelled like vanilla and it took everything in me not to push her head down. I bet she gave some bomb ass head with those full lips she had. And I could tell, even through her uniform, that she had body. Whoever was tappin' that was a lucky man. I could tell she was s freak just by looking at her.

She stepped back and smirked at me in a way that let me know I could've bent her ass over if we were in a different situation.

"Speak so we can make sure everything is working, Mr. McDaniels," she said.

"You know you fine, right," I said, taking my opportunity to let her know I peeped her flirtation.

"Mmph," she said, smiling, "you know you're in here for rape and battery, right?"

"Still don't make you any less fine," I smirked.

"Everything's workin' fine," her partner came in and confirmed, giving me a mean mug. I could tell he used to hit that but wasn't anymore and he wasn't happy about it.

"Cool, where do I sign?"

"You'll get your deal once we get Samson and get him on tape," Officer Taylor said, giving me attitude all of a sudden. I guess she had to play tough now that there was another set of eyes and ears in the room.

"As long as I get my deal," I let them know I wasn't playing.

"You give us what we need and we'll take care of you."

"Aight, let's go."

"Slow your roll," her partner said, "You gotta get him to agree to meet you first."

"Gimme my phone," I ordered.

They handed me my phone and I called the number Samson had been calling me from. I put it on speaker.

"Samson," I said once he answered the phone.

"You better be callin' me to tell me you got my money," he said, his voice sending a chill through me.

"Yeah man, I got it. My ex-bitch gave me back what was mine. Her and her nigga were too proud to spend the shit so I got the whole quarter mil."

"I ain't ask you for the backstory. I told you I ain't care how you got it as long as you got what you owed me. If you'd moved faster, your lil' friend might've lived to get on that Megabus to Florida," he laughed coldly.

"You ain't have to kill Scooter, man," I said, getting sad that my boy had lost his life behind this shit.

"Yeah I did. Blame yourself 'cause you dragged him into this shit. Shoulda been more careful about the company he kept," he said. "But no use crying over spilled blood. Meet me at the Riverfront in an hour. You bring me my shit and you might live to tell your friend's kids about him."

He hung up and I sat there mad as hell. If I wasn't in police custody, I'd kill that motherfucker. But I was gonna make sure he got what the fuck he had comin' to him. The cops had him on tape sayin' he killed Scooter and they said they already had Sheila's mom to testify to him whoopin' her ass, so my work was half-done.

"Now what?" I asked, trying to hide my anger.

"Now we setup at the Riverfront and wait," Officer Taylor said.

"Well, let's go. I'm over this shit."

We rode in an unmarked Nissan Altima to the Riverfront. Officer Taylor had changed into a mini-halter sundress and was gonna pretend to be my woman. She looked so good I thought about trying her while we were out there. Looking at her, I wondered where her gun and cuffs were tucked.

They gave me a duffel bag full of marked cash. It wasn't a quarter mil but we knew Samson's ass wasn't gonna count it out there in the open. They really just needed his ass to show up. The rest was a done dada.

Officer Taylor and I sat on the steps just past the underground tunnel that led to the Riverfront. I watched the water and the Harriet II bobbing on the waves. I remembered the times Tammy would drag me down here to walk and talk. Made me miss her a little bit. There weren't a whole lot of people there, which was a good thing in case Samson decided to get stupid when the cops came for his ass.

I put my hand on her thigh and she looked at me like I was crazy.

"We gotta make this shit believable. I'm a hoe. I wouldn't be out here with somebody as fine as you and be able to keep my hands to myself," I said, smirking.

"Mmm hmmm," she said, not moving my hand.

I slid it further up her leg and under her skirt. There weren't many people watching us. Just her partner with a camera pretending to take pictures, who I wanted to see the role playing, and another set of cops posing as a couple on a date not too far away. They didn't wanna raise suspicion.

Before she could stop me, I had my fingers in her pussy. She tried to stay focused but I could tell she was enjoying it. Knowing we had some time before Samson got there, I laid on top of her, sticking my tongue in her mouth. I knew I was goin' to jail for a while, I might as well get it in. She tensed up like she was about to push me off but knew Samson might be watching and waiting to come up to us, so she didn't wanna do anything that would give us away.

I fingered her hard, three fingers in, stretching her pussy. She was wet and tight. I wanted to feel her. I slid my free hand down and unzipped my pants, replacing my fingers with my dick. She gasped into my mouth and I knew she'd never had a monster like mine before. As far as the other cops could tell, it looked like we were just making out, but I was rockin' her ass like this was the last piece of pussy I was gonna get in my life. Hell, it just might be.

She didn't make a sound because she knew I was wearing a wire but her eyes showed she was loving every second of it. I grabbed her ass and it was as soft as I thought it would be. She tightened her muscles around my dick, bringing me to my nut. I squirted all up in her but didn't move immediately because I didn't wanna give our sneak sex act away.

Ahem. I heard someone clear their throat. I knew it was Samson. She reached down and zipped my pants for me. She was a ride or die kinda bitch. I liked that. Too bad I couldn't make her mine.

"You ain't tell me you was bringin' nobody with you," he said as I turned to face him.

"My bitch kinda clingy. She don't let me go too far without her," I said, smirking. "And when I told her I was comin' to the Riverfront, she thought it would be romantic."

Samson just smirked at me. He knew I had a different hoe for every day of the week. Always had.

"You got me?" he asked, looking at the duffel bag.

"Yep," I said, "that's all you."

"Well, I'll let you get back to your... romance," he said laughing. He picked up the bag and started to walk away. He got halfway down the stairs and turned to face us with a gun drawn.

"Too bad you followed yo' nigga down here, beauty. You're collateral damage now," he said smiling.

Before he could pull the trigger, Officer Taylor pulled a gun that must have been strapped to her back and shot his ass in the leg. Samson fell but not before getting off a shot. The bullet caught me in the neck and I fell, my head in her lap. Her partner ran up to Samson who'd dropped the gun and was bleeding all over the place. He handcuffed him and radioed for the paramedics. I looked at Officer Taylor covered in my blood. I knew I wasn't gonna make it 'til the medics made it to me.

"What's your name?" I whispered.

"Keisha," she said, putting pressure on my wound.

"Keisha," I repeated.

I smiled at her. Her pussy was worth dyin' for. It got dark and I felt my breath getting weak. All I remembered was her face when I let out my last breath.

Beth

I hid in the closet of my apartment waiting for Delilah to come back. Just like I thought, she had Samantha with her. I heard her arguing with some man about shooting Sam and then watched as he almost strangled her to death with his belt. He left her in the room and she cried herself to sleep. I figured I would get some rest and snuggled up against my pile of clothes knowing I probably wouldn't get the opportunity to help Sam until the morning. I was awakened by more arguing. I looked at the screen of my cell phone and saw it was three in the damn morning.

Don't these motherfuckers sleep? I asked myself.

"What did you mean I'm weak like my father, Samson? I'm *your* daughter," Delilah yelled.

I thought she was crazy as hell. I wouldn't dare yell at somebody who'd yoked me up like he had her.

"Your momma fucked my brother when she found out about Samantha's momma. She called it get back but her stupid ass got pregnant. The whole time, I thought you were mine. Then she found out about Tanisha and that she was pregnant and told me you weren't mine. Her stupid ass told me everything and after I murdered my weak, disloyal ass brother, I came back and whooped her ass. I hated you. I hated the betrayal that you represented. And your name, that just made it worse," he said calmly.

"So... I'm your niece? And wait... you said Tanisha was pregnant. So, is Tyrone your son or is Sheila your daughter?" Delilah asked, still yelling.

"You ain't stupid. Do the math. And no. You're not my niece. I called Trell my brother because he was closer to me than my blood, or so I thought. But that nigga was always jealous of me and my come up, even though he was comin' up with me. That wasn't enough for him. He wanted the throne."

Delilah sat on the bed with her head in her hands. She was putting two and two together. I already had. Samantha and Sheila were sisters. And all this time she thought she was being molested by her father, she was just being raped by the man her mother was living with.

"So, we're not related," she said, straddling him on the bed.

I couldn't believe my eyes. Was she really about to fuck this man?

"Nope," he said, smiling and palming her ass.

"Well, the way I see it, you need a cold-blooded bitch on your team. And I'm just the bitch for you. Samson and Delilah, we could take over some shit," she said, sliding out of his lap and onto her knees. Before he could say a word, she had his dick out and down her throat.

I watched through the cracked wooden blinds of the closet door. I was disgusted and certain that she was the craziest bitch I'd ever met in my life. I needed to get Samantha outta here and away from these lunatics as soon as possible. I watched as he grabbed her head and grunted, nutting down her throat before pulling her up and fuckin' her in every position imaginable until they lay sweaty and panting on the bed. When they dozed off, I laid down and went to sleep, hoping not to be discovered before I could get myself and Samantha out of the house.

*****

In the morning, I was awakened by shuffling and saw Delilah get up and run into the bathroom. About a half hour later, she came back in, dressed in one of my Victoria Secret PINK sweat suits. She kissed Samson, waking him up.

"I'm goin' to get breakfast. I'll be back for round two," she said, grinning. She looked like she'd just won the lottery.

"Mmm hmmm," he grunted, smacking her on the ass before she jogged out of the room and he rolled back over, going back to sleep.

I had to pee something terrible but I was just gonna have to hold it because he might kill me if he caught me in the house. I sat there, practicing my Kegels, trying to keep my bladder under control. I couldn't even go back to sleep I had to pee so badly. Then, Samson's phone started ringing. He rolled over and answered it, putting it on speaker.

"Samson," I heard a man say.

"You better be callin' me to tell me you got my money," he said, sounding like he wasn't playing.

"Yeah man, I got it. My ex-bitch gave me back what was mine. Her and her nigga were too proud to spend the shit so I got the whole quarter mil," the dude said. His voice sounded familiar to me.

"I ain't ask you for the backstory. I told you I ain't care how you got it as long as you got what you owed me. If you'd moved faster, your lil' friend might've lived to get on that Megabus to Florida," Samson laughed coldly.

"You ain't have to kill Scooter, man," the man said and I realized it was Tre he was talking to.

"Yeah I did. Blame yourself 'cause you dragged him into this shit. Shoulda been more careful about the company he kept," he said. "But no use crying over spilled blood. Meet me at the Riverfront in half an hour. You bring me my shit and you might live to tell your friend's kids about him."

Samson hung up the phone on Tre and got up out of the bed. He walked out the room and was back shortly after. He put the clothes on that he'd had on the night before and walked towards the front of the house. I heard muffled speech and assumed he was talking to Sam. Then I heard the door open and close. I sat still, giving him time to get in his car and leave. After about fifteen minutes, I made a mad dash to the bathroom. I emptied my bladder, washed my hands, and tiptoed into the living room.

Samantha was laying on the couch with ripped towels wrapped around her right leg as tourniquets and dried blood all around her knee. I needed to get her to the hospital. She was out of it but when she looked up and saw me, she smiled.

"Come on, baby. I gotta get you outta here," I said, leaning down to help her up.

"I can't walk, Beth. This shit hurts so bad. Them pain pills they gave me ain't doin' shit for this pain," she whimpered.

"So we gotta get you outta here and to the hospital. Come on, baby. You can do this."

She looked at me sadly before laying back on the couch. I'd never known her to give up before and I couldn't take it. I started crying before I knew it.

"Sam, I'm not gonna leave you here for these crazy motherfuckers to hurt you anymore! Now get the hell up and let's go get you some help!" I screamed at her.

I was so wrapped up in Sam that I didn't hear the door open and Samson come back in. Next thing I knew, I was being snatched backwards by my hair. I was getting a fuckin' haircut when all this was said and done, damn. I looked up and saw him smiling down at me. Him grabbing me did something to Samantha because she sat up on the couch like she was about to get up. *Now she wants to get her ass up?* I thought to myself, annoyed.

"Let her go, Samson," Sam said, her eyes slits.

"Ohhhh, this is your little girlfriend, huh? Delilah told me she had your nose wide the fuck open. We're only as strong as the thing we're weak for. So, let's see how strong you are, Samantha," he said, like he was teaching her some kinda life lesson. "Beth, you're gonna determine whether or not you and Samantha get outta here alive or whether you're gonna die together."

"Samson, *don't! Please!*" Samantha cried.

"Shut up or I'll make you watch," he spat at her. I already knew what was coming.

"It's ok, baby. You know I'll do anything for you. Just promise me you'll still love me and want me when we get outta here," I said, my eyes pleading with Samantha.

She nodded her head 'yes' and I mouthed 'I love you'. She looked away like she couldn't stand to watch as he stood me up and led me down the hallway by my hair.

Samson wasted no time licking and sucking on my neck. He tried to kiss me and when I turned my head, he grabbed my face and leaned down to whisper in my ear.

"Samantha's my daughter. I ain't gonna hurt her. But you... as far as I'm concerned, you're a dyke bitch who's after her money. So, if you're smart, you'll fuck me like your life depends on it. 'Cause it does," he pulled back and looked at me to make sure I got his meaning.

He leaned back in to kiss me again and I didn't turn away this time. I saw what he was capable of so I decided not to fight him anymore. I kissed him with as much passion as I would have Samantha. I let him undress me and take full inventory of my body before licking and sucking on my neck and breasts. I felt myself getting wet and got angry at my body for betraying me. I didn't want to like it but the sensations were there. He undressed himself and I tried not to notice how beautifully chiseled his body was.

I lay there while he gave me head, talking shit about how much better he gave head than a woman and how he was gonna make me his, until I came involuntarily all over his face. I sucked my juices off his tongue when he climbed on top of me, his long locs falling into my face, and let him fuck me. He was gentler with me than he was with Delilah last night. I moaned just enough to satisfy his ego so he wouldn't hurt me. I did it all for Samantha. I just wanted to get her outta here and to the hospital.

When he finished, nutting all over my ass, he stepped back, as if admiring his handiwork. I turned to look at him and saw Delilah standing in the doorway holding a Hardee's bag. I sucked in my breath, making him turn around. He saw her and turned back to me, dismissing her presence altogether. Her face twisted from hurt to anger and she dropped the bag and stormed off. I was worried she would hurt Samantha but I heard the door open and close and knew she'd left.

"Get dressed and get Samantha and go," he said, putting his clothes back on. "I'm nothing if I'm not a man of my word. But don't get too comfortable 'cause like I said, your tight pussy ass is gonna be mine."

I didn't waste any time getting dressed and running to the front of the house. I pulled Samantha up from the couch and she hung on me like dead weight as I dragged her to the car. I opened the back door and laid her down gently on the back seat. She wouldn't look at me and that added insult to injury. Didn't she know I'd done what I just did for *her*? It was to save our lives so that we could be together. She better fix her face and her fuckin' attitude before we got to the got damn hospital or they were gonna be treating her ass for more than damn gunshot wound.

Delilah

I couldn't believe what I was seeing. Samson had Beth bent over long stroking her and telling her he wanted her to be his woman. *I was his woman!* I dropped the breakfast I'd gone to get his ass and stormed out. I shoulda killed everybody in that fuckin' house but I wanted to get away from there, from them, from everything. When I found out Samson wasn't my father, everything made sense to me. He saw that, even at a young age, I was what he wanted and didn't care what anybody said about it. I hated that I had him locked up. Hated that I hadn't known sooner what I know now or we coulda been running some shit. Now, because of me, Samson had to start over. He had to get the money that Tre wouldn't have been able to steal from him if I hadn't called the cops. The guilt was weighing on me as I drove around the city.

I couldn't be mad at Samson for gettin' ass. He'd been locked up for ten years. I knew once he got all that out his system, it would be just me and him. After all those years, all those women, he had always come back to me. Even now. So I had to get outta my feelings. And I knew I needed to get off these streets. The way MPD got down, they'd pull me over to hit on me, and I couldn't take that chance because I was sure they had an APB out on my ass right now. But I couldn't face Samson right now, especially if Beth and Samantha were still there. I was gonna make him miss me. I bet that would make him get his shit together.

I drove towards downtown and remembered I had the key to the Mojo Lounge building. I parked a few blocks up so no one would know I was in there. I could hide out there 'til shit calmed down. I opened the door and was glad the alarm wasn't on. I looked around with a smirk on my face, realizing they were getting ready for the grand opening. I walked up the stairs to the VIP section and laid across the plush bed we'd put up there for strip parties. I put my phone on silent. I wasn't gonna answer any of Samson's calls when he came lookin' for me, which I knew he would.

I dozed off. I needed to rest. Once Samson got the money from Tre or Samantha, whichever he chose, I was gonna need to be able to drive us out of the state. Me and my baby were gonna start over.

Samson and Delilah, I thought, smiling.

*****

I was awakened by squealing and screaming. I didn't know what the hell was goin' on. I looked over the balcony and saw the dude Ron I'd drugged and fucked on one knee. I hid so they couldn't see me and listened.

"Nel, these last couple of months have made me happier than I could have ever imagined. You are such a strong, kind woman. You put everyone else before yourself. I know I asked you the other night and you said yes but I wanted to do this shit the right way. I asked for your hand from your brother and he gave me his blessing. Jeff gave his as well. I told you when I met you that we were gonna be the King and Queen but now we're movin' to bigger thangs and are gonna take the A by storm. Will you do me the honor of being Mrs. Blowemup?" he asked her.

Sheila was in tears. She looked sick. I found joy in thinking that the bitch could be dying or something. I mean, why else would anyone wanna marry her trash ass? I looked around and Tyrone had Tammy wrapped up with his hands on her stomach. He was smiling from ear-to-ear but she looked uncomfortable, like his touch was unwelcome. Anthony was there, looking like a sad ass puppy dog. After all the shit he'd done wrong, he still had feelings for Sheila's ass. He wasn't even trying to hide the shit.

I was surprised to see Beth there grinning like she was a part of the family or some shit. I figured she would still be somewhere with Samson waist deep in her ass. I guess he let her and his precious Samantha go and she was here in Sam's place 'cause I shot her ass. I'm surprised Ron ain't wanna whoop her ass because she helped me drug and fuck his ass. Next to her was Shawn's fine ass looking like a chocolate Popsicle. I wanted to mount his ass right then and there.

I decided to throw a wrench in Sheila and Ron's happy moment. I walked over to my purse and pulled out my nine. I tucked it into my sweatpants so that it was visible. Walking down the stairs, I did a slow clap, making them all turn around.

"Well... well... well... look who found her knight in shining armor. I mean, I've had the dick so I really think you're settling, Sheila," I laughed, pulling my gun out of my pants. "Anthony is a much better fuck. But, I guess you take what you can get, huh?"

I pointed my gun at her. All this time. All the work I'd put in, I'd be damned if this bitch got to live a happy life and I was dealin' with Samson's wandering dick ass.

Ron

I saw the look on Sheila's face when I told her I had some things to handle and would be back to get her. I loved how she didn't question me. Even with all that had happened, she was still willing to trust me. I knew I was making the right decision. I went to Tyrone's house to scoop him and Jeff so I could take them to lunch and then, hopefully ring shopping.

"Whattup Ty?" I asked, dapping him up. "Jeff?" I said, doing the same.

"Tammy in there sleep. The baby ok. But she's not dealin' with what happened too well. I can't really touch her without her damn near jumpin' outta her skin. Seein' Jeff seemed to make her feel better, though," he said, smiling down at his nephew.

"Damn man, I'm sorry. Y'all gone get through this shit, though. It's just gonna take some time and a lil' counseling. Y'all ready to go grub?" I asked as we got in my car.

"Yeah! Uncle Ty wouldn't let me eat nothin' so I'm starving," Jeff said, getting in the back seat.

"Where you wanna go, Jeff? You pick," I said, looking at him in my rearview mirror while I backed out.

"I don't know. Can we go to Popeye's?" he asked, not knowing the seriousness of the conversation we were about to have.

"Really? Popeye's?" I asked, laughing.

"Yes sir. That's what I want. Is that ok?"

"Sure is. Let's go to Popeye's," I headed towards the Boulevard.

When we got to the restaurant, I gave Jeff a twenty so he could get what he wanted. I wasn't hungry. I was too nervous to be. Tyrone decided not to eat anything, either. We sat at the table waiting for Jeff. I didn't want to start without him. Jeff came to the table with chicken tenders with mashed potatoes and gravy and a sweet tea. He sat down and dove right in.

"I wanted to talk to y'all because you're the two most important men in Nel's life. I asked her to marry me and she said yes," I said and Jeff stopped eating and looked at me with a huge smile on his face.

"Word?" he said.

I nodded. Tyrone sat back in his seat. He was hiding a smile because he knew there was more coming. We'd already talked about this but I wanted to get his formal approval. This meeting was really more for Jeff's benefit. I always wanted him to know he had a say-so in things.

"I gotta job offer in Atlanta and she's agreed to come with me. I wanted to see how y'all felt about that because, if I don't get your blessing then this won't feel right. Jeff, I want you to move with us but that means leaving your friends and school and starting over," I turned to him.

"You make my momma happy. I want her to be happy. And I hate that school so leavin' ain't a big deal for me. But I don't know about leaving Grandma Tanisha when she's sick and Grandma Julianne. How does Momma feel about that?" he asked. I liked that he was so considerate of everyone else. Sheila had done a great job with him.

"She's ready to go. Atlanta is only two hours away so she's not worried about bein' too far from everyone," I explained. That seemed to be a good enough answer because he went back to eating. "And Ty, I wanted to ask you for her hand. You know I love your sister and she respects you. I wouldn't feel right marrying her without your approval."

Tyrone kept staring at me. He had a smirk on his face like he was enjoying being able to decide whether or not I would be able to marry his sister. I sat there and let him have his moment. We'd grown close over the past few weeks, especially after everything that had gone on with our women.

"Man, you know you got my blessing. You came into the picture and have taken care of Nel while she's sick. You kick it with nephew here," he said, nudging Jeff who was grubbin' so hard he probably hadn't heard a word I'd said to Tyrone. "And you stuck around even with all this drama that was goin' on. You were down to ride for me and for my wife when that shit went down at the house and woulda beat the fuck outta Samson if he'd moved wrong."

I smiled, grateful to hear I had the green light from the both of them. I could breathe easier. When Jeff was done eating, we went to Kay Jewelers to pick out Nel's ring. I spent my entire commission from the Mojo Lounge on it because she was worth that and more to me. When I dropped Jeff and Tyrone back off, it had been well over an hour since I'd taken Sheila to the hospital to see Tanisha. I pulled out my phone and saw several missed calls from her. I'd put my phone on silent during her meeting this morning and had been so caught up in getting ready for the official proposal that I hadn't taken my phone off silent. I called her.

"Where the hell are you, Ron? I been callin' you. I'm tired and wanted to take a nap before the meeting this afternoon. You know how serious I am about my naps," she yelled into the phone.

"Baby my phone was still on silent from the meeting this morning." I explained, trying not to laugh because the woman was truly serious about her naps. "I'm on my way now. I'll be at the hospital in like 5 minutes. You still got time to take a nap."

She hung up the phone and I knew I was in trouble. I wanted to just give her the ring when I picked her up and tell her where I was but that would've ruined the surprise. I was gonna do this right and propose in the venue that brought us together.

I pulled up and Sheila was standing outside with her hands crossed over her chest looking mad as hell. I wanted to laugh but knew better. I wasn't trying to go to war with this woman. She had a mouth like a razor.

I drove us to her house and the car was completely silent. Yeah, she was mad. When we got to the house, she didn't even wait for me to open her car door for her. She got out, slamming the door, and stomped to the house. I shook my head at the fact that, even though she was weak from the chemo, she still had the energy to give me attitude. I got out, walking to the house. I turned the knob and laughed.

"She locked the fuckin' door," I said to no one.

I thought about using my key and going in but decided to go home and lay down myself. I really wasn't in the mood to deal with her shit when I knew I didn't do anything wrong. I knew she'd be calling me fussing about the fact that I didn't come in before I got home. I got on the I-65 ramp headed to Prattville and my phone started ringing. I laughed to myself when I answered the phone.

"Yes bae," I said, a smile in my voice.

"You left?" she whined.

"You locked the door so I figured you wanted to be alone."

"I can't believe you left. You know I didn't want you to leave," she pouted, sounding like a spoiled child.

"How was I supposed to know that? Your actions said somethin' else," I said, being honest. I wasn't gonna spend the rest of my life tending to her spoiled ass. I would spoil her, yeah, but she wasn't gonna act spoiled.

"Man, just come back," she said, like it was that easy. It really was, but just because she was making demands, I wasn't gonna let her know that.

"Nel, I'm already at the house," I lied. "I'll come get you at two for the meeting. Make sure you get something to eat and take your nap, ok."

"Fine! Whatever, Ron!" She hung up the phone.

I laughed as I took my exit. *Check and mate*, I thought.

*****

I pulled up to Sheila's house at two on the dot. I didn't know what to expect because she didn't get her way earlier. I walked in, ready for anything.

"Nel!" I called out to her. "Come on, we gotta go."

I walked through the house looking for her because she hadn't responded. When I walked into her bedroom and she was laying in her bed, naked. I smiled knowin' what she had in mind.

"We got time," she smiled at me, spreading her legs and rubbing on her clit.

I didn't argue with that. I slid my feet out of my shoes and took off my shirt. I unbuttoned and pulled off my pants. I got on my knees and slid her to the edge of the bed. I couldn't lie. I missed her. But I never pressured her to because I knew that her body was going through a lot with the treatment and her health was more important to me than sex.

"You sure? You need your strength," I said, even though I hoped she wouldn't stop me.

"I'm ok, bae. Please. I miss you," she looked down at me with a pained look on her face.

I didn't say another word. I went to work eating her until she came all over my face. But this time, unlike in her office, I stood up and eased into her, pulling her legs onto my shoulders. She let out a loud moan that sent a chill through me. She felt so good I was about to explode. I leaned down to kiss her to distract myself, pushing her legs back and going even deeper. She started to whimper in that way that would make any man lose his mind. But I was worried that I was hurting her so I stopped and looked her in the face to make sure it was pleasure she was feeling.

"Why'd you stop?" she yelled at me, looking at me like I was crazy.

I didn't respond. I just dug back into her, trying to break her back. I stroked and sweated, pausing to suck on her tongue, her neck, her breasts. She had her "I love you" melody on repeat and I was beating her pussy up as the bass line. She kept tightening around my dick, shivering and cumming. Wrapping her legs around me, she lifted her ass up and started grinding me from below. I held it together as long as I could before letting potential my sons and daughters race for their chance at creation.

I rolled off of her, not wanting to lay my weight on top of her and she turned to me, pulling my locs out of my face so that she could kiss me on the cheek.

"I love you so much," she said, laying back down to catch her breath. "I'm sorry for how I acted earlier."

That's what I needed to hear. I smiled and got up to wash up.

"Hey, come on. We're gonna be late," I said, walking into the bathroom.

She joined me and we cleaned ourselves up before dressing and getting into the car to leave. We got to the Lounge at two fifteen. Shawn, Anthony, Tammy, and Tyrone were already inside. Nel told me that Beth was coming as Samantha's proxy because she'd been shot. Neither one of us had to say that we knew Delilah was behind that shit. We sat, waiting for Beth to arrive. Tyrone kept smiling at me because he knew I was gonna propose to her here. Tammy looked like she was somewhere else mentally. I knew she was still getting over what Tre had done to her. Anthony kept eyeballin' me. I knew he still had feelings for Sheila and hated that I was with her. He was really gonna hate my ass when I presented this rock.

"Hi..." Beth said, coming through the door.

I looked at her and decided not to say anything about the fact that she'd helped Delilah drug and rape me. I figured if she was there for Samantha, she had gotten away from Delilah. And knowing how manipulative Delilah was just from my one encounter with her, I didn't hold it against the girl. I remembered the way that pussy felt though, even though I was out of it. I had to keep myself from smiling at the thought.

"Hey Beth. Thank you for joining us today. I wanted to meet with all of you to go over the details of the Grand Opening of the Mojo Lounge next week. Shawn has the list of events and I wanted to sit down and review them together so that we can make sure that they're to your satisfaction," Sheila said as Shawn handed out the events proposal.

"Before you go any further, Nel," Tyrone interrupted her, "I wanna talk to Anthony and was hoping to speak with Samantha about buying me out of the Lounge."

He wrapped his arms around Tammy from behind and waited for a response. Anthony smirked and Beth looked confused.

"We're about to have a child and I just don't think that this is the best move for us anymore. And the fact that Delilah is still a partner doesn't make things any better. So, Anthony, Beth, are either of you interested?" he finished.

"Let me call Samantha and see how she feels about it," Beth said, walking outside to get on her phone.

Almost simultaneously, Nel's phone rang. She looked at the caller ID and smiled broadly.

"Excuse me, I have to take this. Y'all sit down and get comfortable. I'll be right back."

She walked towards the back and I heard excitement in her voice. I knew she'd just gotten some good news. I wondered what it was. Even though she told us to sit down, no one moved. Beth came back in all smiles. So did Nel.

"Tyrone, Sam said she'd love to buy your part of the Lounge. She offered fifteen thousand. Is that enough?"

"Yeah, that would be fine. We'll set up a meeting to discuss everything," Tyrone responded.

"No need. She's got her attorney drafting the paperwork now and we'll be in touch when it's ready. I'll get your information before I leave and we can meet at her attorney's office to finalize everything."

This white girl is a beast, I thought to myself laughing. *I ain't mad at her, though.*

Tyrone nodded and looked down at Tammy who gave him a weak smile. I knew they were happy to be getting out of this situation.

"That's great! I have some awesome news as well. I just got the call that I've been waiting for and Shawn is now going to be managing the Urban Department of

Vantech. I'll be moving to Atlanta with this handsome guy and have been given the green light to open our new branch. Shawn has been my right hand for some time now and I know that he will do a great job with marketing the Lounge for you all," she beamed at Shawn.

He smiled from ear-to-ear and I was proud of her and him. I knew that this was my chance. I looked at Nel and smiled.

"What's up, bae?" she asked.

"Well, first of all, congratulations to you and to Shawn. I'm happy that situation worked out. But there's one more thing that needs to be said before we close this meeting out," I said, getting down on one knee.

Nel squealed and Tammy gave the first real smile I'd seen since the Tre situation. Beth even screamed. I guess all women got excited when a man got down on one knee. I wasted no time.

"Nel, these last couple of months have made me happier than I could have ever imagined. You are such a strong, kind woman. You put everyone else before yourself. I know I asked you the other night and you said yes but I wanted to do this shit the right way. I asked for your hand from your brother and he gave me his blessing. Jeff gave his as well. I told you when I met you that we were gonna be the King and Queen but now we're movin' to bigger thangs and are gonna take the A by storm. Will you do me the honor of being Mrs. Blowemup?" I said, pulling the ring box out of my pants pocket and opening it.

Nel started crying as I put the ring on her finger. It was a five carat solitaire that I knew would look great on her petite hand.

Before she could respond we heard a noise coming from the stairs. All of us looked up to see Delilah's ass slow-clapping as she made her way down the stairs, a gun tucked into the waist of her jogging pants.

"Well... well... well... look who found her knight in shining armor. I mean, I've had the dick so I really think you're settling, Sheila," she said laughing, pulling the gun out of her pants. "Anthony is a much better fuck. But, I guess you take what you can get, huh?"

She pointed the gun at Nel and I stood up in front of her, my body blocking Delilah's shot.

"I don't give a fuck who gets this bullet, you or her," she said to me. "Either way ain't gone be no damn wedding."

Then she started waving the gun around, pointing it at everyone in the room.

"Y'all having this meeting without me like I'm not a partner in this business. Like you can treat me like an afterthought. Trying to get lawyers to push me outta this agreement. Y'all motherfuckas stuck with me. Or I'll just handle all of y'all and run this bitch on my own."

I didn't move. Tyrone was shielding Tammy as well. This bitch was outta her mind. I felt Nel's hand on my back. She slowly lifted my shirt and I knew she was going for my gun. I didn't move. My baby was a rider for real. I knew she was tired of Delilah and I gave Tyrone a look to let him know what was about to happen.

Tyrone

When Ron dropped Jeff and I back at the house, I couldn't wait to tell Tammy the news. Jeff went into the spare bedroom to watch TV and I walked into our bedroom to find Tammy laying in the bed, balled up. I'd gotten rid of the bed that Tre had raped her in and gotten a new one delivered just this morning because I knew she wouldn't be able to sleep in that damn bed. But, worse than the bed, Tre had taken my wife's spirit. She had been walking around in a daze since they'd released her from the hospital. I knew she was glad that Tre was locked up but she felt like she would never really be free of him as long as he was alive.

I sat on the bed and looked at her.

"Hey baby. You eat?" I asked.

"I'm not hungry, Ty," she said without turning around to look at me.

"I know but you need to eat. You gotta take the medicine they gave you," I said as gently as I could.

Inside I was seething. We'd just gotten married. Just found out we were having a son. And now my wife was battling a depression and fear of a nigga I was supposed to be protecting her from. I felt like a failure.

She got up from the bed without another word and walked into the kitchen. I didn't follow her. I knew she needed her space. When she walked back into the bedroom, she sat down with her turkey sandwich and glass of water and looked at me.

"I'm gonna have to face him in court, baby. I don't ever wanna see him again but I'm gonna have to face him in court and tell them what he did to me. I just can't do it!"

"Then don't," I said, knowing that they had a strong enough case to lock his ass up for a while. "I'm worried about your health. We're gonna get you some counseling and make sure you're ok. Let the legal system do its job. They have enough to keep his ass caged up, baby."

"You mean it? I thought you'd be mad at me for not wanting to face him," she said, looking relieved.

"I mean it. Every word of it," I said, leaning over to kiss her cheek.

She flinched and that hurt me. I knew it would be a while before I could love on my wife the way I wanted to. Just that reality made me wanna murder Tre myself. I watched Tammy eat her sandwich but it looked like it was hurting her. I would never know the full scope of the damage that he'd done to her. I walked out of the room and went outside to smoke a Newport. I needed to calm down. I couldn't take my anger out on her for what he'd done to her. And I couldn't let her see me angry because she might think it was something that she'd done. I lit my Newport and my phone started ringing. I looked at the caller ID and didn't recognize the number.

"Hello?" I answered hesitantly.

"Mr. Price?" a woman's voice came over the phone.

"Yes," I said, thinking it was a bill collector.

"This is Officer Taylor. I wanted to call you personally to tell you that Tremaine McDaniels was murdered today. He was shot by Samson Powell in an attempt to help us bring him to custody. I thought you and your wife would want to know this and that it would give you all some kind of peace. I hope it does anyway."

I had to admit that the news was great. I needed to know that Tre couldn't harm Tammy anymore. But then the reality sank in that I had to tell my nephew that his dad was dead. I didn't know which to do first. I really thought that it was his mother's place to tell him so I called Nel.

"Hey baby girl. Did I wake you up?" I asked when I heard the grogginess in her voice when she answered the phone.

"Yeah. But you're good. I need to be gettin' up anyway. Ron should be on his way to get me in a lil' bit for the meeting at the Lounge. Y'all still gonna make it, right? How's Tammy doing?"

"Whoa, slow down," I said, laughing at her mind and how it always seemed to be going a hundred miles a minute. "I called with some bad news but yeah we'll be there at two thirty and Tammy is still dealing with what happened. It's gonna take some time for her to get over it mentally and physically."

"Well, I know with a husband like you, she'll be just fine," she smiled into the phone. "But what's the bad news?"

"I just got a call from the Officer who arrested Tre. She said he was killed when he tried to help the police apprehend Samson. You know Jeff's over here with me but I feel like you should be the one to tell him."

She sighed heavily but it seemed more a sigh of relief. I held the phone and waited for her response. After a good five minutes or so, she spoke.

"Well... I guess I'll have to tell him. But not now. I'll figure out the best way to break it to him. Right now, let's focus on what's important and what we can control. I'll see y'all at the Lounge. Are you bringing Jeff with you or taking him back to my foster mother's?"

I was a bit thrown off my her response to her son's father being dead, but he had just held her at gunpoint and raped my wife, so I guess her response could be understood.

"We'll take him to Julianne's on the way to the Lounge. I just wanted to tell you the news. I haven't told Tammy yet. I think I'll wait to tell her tonight," I admitted.

"Sounds like a plan. I'll tell Jeff tonight, too. I'll fill Ron in this afternoon and we'll figure out how to break it to him."

"Cool. See you in a lil' while. Love you."

"Love you, too, Ty. See you soon."

I didn't feel the need to tell her about my wanting out of the Lounge right now. We all had so much goin' on. And I wanted to make the announcement in front of Anthony and Samantha so that they'd have the option to buy me out before I sought out someone else. I had a couple of guys from the job who were definitely interested in the opportunity.

"Jeff!" I called, walking back into the house.

"Yes sir," he yelled back coming out of the spare room.

"You ready? We're gonna take you to Julianne's before we go to our business meeting."

"Yes sir," he said looking disappointed. I knew he wanted to stay at the house but with all of the craziness that had been going on, I didn't want to risk anything happening to him.

I went into the bedroom and Tammy was getting dressed. The man in me wanted to grab her and toss her on the bed and have my way with her. But I knew better. It would be months before I could have my wife the way I wanted to again. I pressed down my erection and just stood in the doorway watching her pull on her leggings and tank top. I couldn't wait for her body to get swollen with my child and massage her feet and run out in the middle of the night to get some stupid combination of things that she was craving.

She looked up at me smiling at her and smiled back. That made me feel better. I missed my Tammy. She was truly my best friend.

"You ready, beautiful?" I asked, holding me hand out to her.

"Yeah," she said, sheepishly.

She walked over and took my hand. We walked into the living room and she, Jeff, and I got into the truck headed to drop him off and onto the meeting. We pulled up in front of Julianne's house and she was working in her garden. She had on a sun hat and looked really involved in pulling those weeds up. When she heard the car pull into the driveway, she stood up and removed her gloves.

"Hey y'all!" she said, smiling and walking over to the truck.

Tammy and I got out of the truck with Jeff. He hugged us and kissed her before running into the house. I guess he was trying to avoid having to help with yardwork.

"Y'all doin' ok?" she asked, looking back and forth from me to Tammy who looked to the ground.

"We will be," I said, leaning down and kissing her on the cheek.

"Everything is a day-by-day process. Every day will be a step towards healing," she said, looking at Tammy and lifting her face up by her chin so she could look into her eyes.

"I know. It's just hard," Tammy admitted.

"Life is hard, baby. But as long as you're still living you have the opportunity to be ok," she said smiling at me. "And with a handsome man like this by your side who loves your every mole and laugh line, I know you're gonna be just fine."

"Now, are you gonna tell me what news your sister called me about or are you gonna tell me I gotta wait, too," she asked me, laughing because my face told her I wasn't gonna tell her a thing.

"Fine. I taught Nel patience, I guess it's my turn to practice some, huh?"

"Unfortunately, yes ma'am," I grinned.

"Well gone then. You haven't served me any purpose," she laughed, hugging me and Tammy before we got back in the truck to leave.

"So, who told her what happened to me? Does the entire universe know?" Tammy asked me angrily as we pulled off.

"Woman stop that mess. You know Nel was gonna tell her what was goin' on. She didn't mean no harm by it. Why're you actin' like that?"

"I mean, would you want the world to know about the time you got raped in prison?" she shot at me, hitting a nerve.

"Really Tammy? You attacking me like I did something to you? Like I can't relate to how the fuck you feelin' right now? Well, I can *because* I was violated in prison. The difference between me and you is that Samson did that shit to me and he's out and fuckin' my momma now. Just beat the hell outta her and let Delilah stab her almost to death. But you get the relief of the motherfucka that you let beat and rape you for *years* bein' dead so he'll never come looking for you again," I said then got pissed at myself for letting that shit slip in anger.

"Tremaine's dead?" Tammy said and a look of joyful ease came over her face.

"Yeah, I got a call from Officer Taylor earlier telling me that he was killed helping them catch Samson. Samson shot him," I went ahead and told her.

"So Tre's dead and Samson is locked up but Delilah's ass is still running around here somewhere," she said, the ease leaving her face as quickly as it came. "She's more dangerous than either of them!"

"They'll get her, baby," I promised, hoping I wasn't lying.

"Well, at least two of their asses are gone. I wonder where Scooter is."

"I don't know. But no one has seen or heard from him so hopefully he's gone on about his business. I'd hate to kill him," I said, meaning every word.

We pulled up to the Lounge and got out just as Shawn was walking up to the door with Anthony. I didn't see Nel or Ron's car so I wondered what was holding them up. We went in and I dapped Shawn up and gave Anthony a head nod before we all looked around at the setup. I was impressed by it. Too bad I was getting out of the business because I had a hundred ideas about how to make this spot the go-to for everything from business luncheons to parties. Maybe I'd tell Nel about them and she could pass the word on.

Nel and Ron walked in not too long after we got there. We all greeted one another and I found myself looking around for Samantha.

"Can we get started?" Anthony asked, giving Ron the side eye.

"We're waiting on one more person," Nel said, more to the rest of us than to him. "Let's have a seat. She should be here shortly."

We sat down obediently. You could cut the tension with a knife. It wasn't made any better when Beth walked in the door, all smiles and greeted us, "Hi..."

Nel wasted no time getting to business once she arrived, "Hey Beth. Thank you for joining us today. I wanted to meet with all of you to go over the details of the Grand Opening of the Mojo Lounge next week. Shawn has the list of events and I wanted to sit down and review them together so that we can make sure that they're to your satisfaction."

Shawn handed out the events proposal. I saw this as my opportunity.

"Before you go any further, Nel," I interrupted her, "I wanna talk to Anthony and was hoping to speak with Samantha about buying me out of the Lounge."

I wrapped my arms around Tammy from behind and waited for a response. Anthony smirked and Beth looked confused.

"We're about to have a child and I just don't think that this is the best move for us anymore. And the fact that Delilah is still a partner doesn't make things any better. So, Anthony, Beth, are either of you interested?" I finished.

"Let me call Samantha and see how she feels about it," Beth said, walking outside to get on her phone.

Almost simultaneously, Nel's phone rang. She looked at the caller ID.

"Excuse me, I have to take this. Y'all sit back down and get comfortable. I'll be right back."

She walked towards the back. Even though she told us to sit down, no one moved. Beth came back with excitement on her face. So did Nel.

"Tyrone, Sam said she'd love to buy your part of the Lounge. She offered fifteen thousand. Is that enough?" Beth said.

"Yeah, that would be fine. We'll set up a meeting to discuss everything," I responded.

"No need. She's got her attorney drafting the paperwork now and we'll be in touch when they're ready. I'll get your information before I leave and we can meet at her attorney's office to finalize everything."

I nodded and looked down at Tammy who gave me a weak smile. I knew she was still battling with the news of Tre's death. And I knew she felt bad about bringing up that prison shit. She was the only person who knew about it and she knew that was the one time that I felt like less than a man and had led to my attempted suicide when I was locked up. But I wasn't gonna hold it against her. She had acted out of emotion.

"That's great! I have some awesome news as well. I just got the call that I've been waiting for and Shawn is now going to be managing the Urban Department of Vantech. I'll be moving to Atlanta with this handsome guy," she said looking over at Ron, "and have been given the green light to open our new branch. Shawn has been my right hand for some time now and I know that he will do a great job with marketing the Lounge for you all," she beamed at Shawn.

Shawn smiled from ear-to-ear and I saw Ron mentally preparing to make his move. Nel must have seen it, too, because she wrinkled her forehead.

"What's up, bae?" she asked him.

"Well, first of all, congratulations to you and to Shawn. I'm happy that situation worked out. But there's one more thing that needs to be said before we close this meeting out," he said, getting down on one knee.

Nel squealed and Tammy seemed to forget everything that had happened to her because she smiled like she was being proposed to. Beth even screamed. I laughed at all the women in the room getting all excited and Anthony looked like someone had just punched his ass in the stomach.

"Nel, these last couple of months have made me happier than I could have ever imagined. You are such a strong, kind woman. You put everyone else before yourself. I know I asked you the other night and you said yes but I wanted to do this shit the right way. I asked for your hand from your brother and he gave me his blessing. Jeff gave his as well. I told you when I met you that we were gonna be the King and Queen but now we're movin' to bigger thangs and are gonna take the A by storm. Will you do me the honor of being Mrs. Blowemup?" Ron said, pulling the ring box out of his pants pocket and opening it.

Nel started crying.

Before Nel could answer, I looked up and saw Delilah walking down the stairs doin' a slow clap. I wanted to run and tackle her ass to the ground but she pulled her gun out of her pants.

"Well... well... well... look who found her knight in shining armor. I mean, I've had the dick so I really think you're settling, Sheila," she said laughing. "Anthony is a much better fuck. But, I guess you take what you can get, huh?"

She pointed the gun at Nel and Ron stepped in front of her, blocking Delilah's shot.

"I don't give a fuck who gets this bullet, you or her," she said to Ron. "Either way ain't gone be no damn wedding."

Then she started waving the gun around, pointing it at everyone in the room.

"Y'all having this meeting without me like I'm not a partner in this business. Like you can treat me like an afterthought. Trying to get lawyers to push me outta this agreement. Y'all motherfuckas stuck with me. Or I'll just handle all of y'all and run this bitch on my own."

I eased Tammy behind me as well and looked at Anthony whose punk ass looked like a deer caught in headlights. Then I looked from Shawn to Beth to Ron and all of them looked like they were ready for war. Ron gave me a look that I knew. Nel was behind him and from the angle I was standing at, it looked like she had his shirt up. My baby sister had finally had enough. But I was ready just in case she missed. Delilah wasn't getting outta here alive. Some of us may have to take a hit, too, but we were willing to take that chance.

Tammy

I didn't feel like living after what Tre did to me. Tyrone was doing everything that he could to make me comfortable. Hell, he had a new bed delivered to the house so I didn't have to sleep in the bed that I was raped in. I still couldn't stand being touched though, and I knew it was fuckin' with my husband. He had to make me eat so I could take the antibiotics that they gave me at the hospital to kill any STI Tre may have given me. They said it wasn't gonna hurt the baby and if I contracted anything that would be worse on the baby than anything but all I could think was that for the next seven days, I would be reminded what happened to me twice a day.

And now Tyrone was talking about me going to counseling to talk about the shit. I just wanted to forget that it ever happened. Tre had done worse to me. I just thought, now that I was married to Tyrone I would be safe from this kinda shit. And he did come and save me but I couldn't help but be mad at him for not getting here sooner. I know there was nothing he could do. It's not like the man was psychic or anything, but I just wish he could have prevented it all from happening. Hell, maybe I did need counseling.

He came back in from wherever the hell he and Jeff had gone with Ron. I didn't care to ask. I knew I was being selfish but I had the right to be. He sat down on the bed where I was curled up in the fetal position.

"Hey baby. You eat?" he asked.

"I'm not hungry, Ty."

"I know but you need to eat. You gotta take the medicine they gave you."

There he was making me take them damn pills again. I got up from the bed and stormed into the kitchen and made a damn turkey sandwich. I had a glass of water with me too, so I could take the fuckin' antibiotics. I ate my food in silence and he handed me the pill bottle when I was done. I swallowed the pill down and finished the water so I could wash it down. I finally looked at Ty and decided to share my thoughts.

"I'm gonna have to face him in court, baby. I don't ever wanna see him again but I'm gonna have to face him in court and tell them what he did to me. I just can't do it!"

"Then don't. I'm worried about your health. We're gonna get you some counseling and make sure you're ok. Let the legal system do its job. They have enough to keep his ass caged up, baby."

"You mean it? I thought you'd be mad at me for not wanting to face him," I said, so happy he wasn't gonna make me testify.

"I mean it. Every word of it," he leaned over to kiss my cheek.

I flinched and a pained look came over his face. I felt so bad about making him feel this way. It was involuntary, though. He got up and walked outside. I knew he was going to smoke. I took the time to cry. I walked into the bathroom and locked the door. I had been doing this several times a day. I knew part of it was pregnancy hormones. But the other part... the other part was being violated again by the man I had given so many years to. I cried for all the time I spent trying to love Tre. I loved him hoping that it would be contagious and he'd love me back. But it wasn't. The more I loved him, the more he hated me. I guess because I loved him regardless of what he did.

Then I meet Tyrone and he loved me so honestly. Even now when he'd watched Tre fuckin' me with his child inside of me. And I was being so cruel to him but I couldn't help it. I was gonna do better by my husband. He deserved it. Our child deserves it. Hell, I deserve it after being treated like shit for so long.

I cleaned up my face and started to get dressed when I heard Tyrone come in the house and yell for Jeff to get ready to go to Julianne's house. I felt Ty's presence in the doorway before I turned around and saw him. I took my time so that he could at least get to look at me since I wasn't letting him touch me and God only knew when I would be ok with being touched again.

Once I had on my tank, leggings, and sandals, I looked over at him and smiled. He smiled back and I know my smile had made his day.

"You ready, beautiful?" he asked.

"Yeah," I said softly.

I walked over and took his hand and the three of us got into the truck. I knew Jeff wanted to stay at the house but Delilah's crazy ass was still roaming the city somewhere so we couldn't take that chance. For the life of me, I couldn't figure out why she hadn't left yet. She really was crazy as hell.

When we got to Julianne's house and she was working in her garden. She had on a sun hat and looked like she should've been on the cover of somebody's Home and Garden magazine. When she saw us, she got up and walked over to the truck, pulling her gloves off and dropping them in her flower bed.

"Hey y'all!" she said, a huge smile on her face.

Ty and I got out of the truck with Jeff. He hugged us and kissed her before running into the house.

"Y'all doin' ok?" she asked, her eyes landing on me. I looked off hoping she couldn't see the pain in my eyes.

"We will be," Ty said, leaning down and kissing her on the cheek.

"Everything is a day-by-day process. Every day will be a step towards healing," she said, and lifted my face with her hand.

"I know. It's just hard," I admitted.

"Life is hard, baby. But as long as you're still living you have the opportunity to be ok," she said smiling at me. "And with a handsome man like this by your side who loves your every mole and laugh line, I know you're gonna be just fine."

"Now, are you gonna tell me what news your sister called me about or are you gonna tell me I gotta wait, too," she asked Ty and they shared a laugh. I had no idea what they were talking about so I stared at her garden. It was pretty. I wanted a garden. Maybe it would give me something to occupy my mind.

"Fine. I taught Nel patience, I guess it's my turn to practice some, huh?"

"Unfortunately, yes ma'am," Ty grinned.

"Well gone then. You haven't served me any purpose," she laughed, hugging me and Ty before we got back in the truck to leave.

"So, who told her what happened to me? Does the entire universe know?" I asked, pissed off.

"Woman stop that mess. You know Nel was gonna tell her what was goin' on. She didn't mean no harm by it. Why're you actin' like that?"

"I mean, would you want the world to know about the time you got raped in prison?" I shot at him, regretting it as soon as I'd said it.

"Really Tammy? You attacking me like I did something to you? Like I can't relate to how the fuck you feelin' right now. Well, I can *because* I was violated in prison. The difference between me and you is that Samson did that shit to me and he's out and fuckin' my momma now. Just beat the hell outta her and let Delilah stab her almost to death. But you get the relief of the motherfucka that you let beat and rape you for *years* bein' dead so he'll never come looking for you again," he yelled at me.

My eyes got big. *Did he just say Tre was dead?* I thought to myself. I wanted to jump for joy and cry at the same time.

"Tremaine's dead?" I asked him, making sure I heard him right.

"Yeah, I got a call from Officer Taylor earlier telling me that he was killed helping them catch Samson. Samson shot him," he confirmed.

"So Tre's dead and Samson is locked up but Delilah's ass is still running around here somewhere," I pauded. "She's more dangerous than both of them."

"They'll get her, baby," he said but I knew that there was no way for him to be sure of that shit.

"Well, at least two of their asses are gone. I wonder where Scooter is."

"I don't know. But no one has seen or heard from him so hopefully he's gone on about his business. I'd hate to kill him," Ty said, with bass in his voice.

I loved the way he got defensive when it came to me. We pulled up to the Lounge and Shawn and Anthony were on their way inside. I wondered where Nel was.

Usually she would've beat us there. I hoped she was feeling okay. We walked in and were looking around when she and Ron walked into the building. I had an eerie feeling. Maybe it was just everything connected to this business venture. I was glad Ty had agreed to get out of the whole situation. I was ready for him to tell them so we could go. After that, there'd be no reason for us to be there.

I looked at Tyrone and realized he was looking for Samantha. I felt a way about that but I had to trust that it was solely for business purposes. We all stood around and waited for her to get started. Apparently, Anthony couldn't wait.

"Can we get started?" Anthony looked at Ron all ugly. I had to hide my laugh. That nigga was pitiful. All the shit he'd done and he was still all in his feelings about Nel being with somebody else.

"We're waiting on one more person," Nel said, more to the rest of us than to him. "Let's have a seat. She should be here shortly."

We sat down. It was so tense in the room and something was telling me that something wasn't right but I couldn't put my finger on it so I didn't say anything. The door opened and Beth walked in.

"Hi..." she said, looking nervous but tried to hide it behind a smile. Her lip and eye looked like she was healing from a serious ass whoopin'. I wondered if it was from Delilah or Sam.

Nel wasted no time getting to business after that, which let me know she knew Beth was coming.

"Hey Beth. Thank you for joining us today. I wanted to meet with all of you to go over the details of the Grand Opening of the Mojo Lounge next week. Shawn has the list of events and I wanted to sit down and review them together so that we can make sure that they're to your satisfaction."

Shawn handed out the events proposal and Ty spoke up.

"Before you go any further, Nel," my husband interrupted her, "I wanna talk to Anthony and was hoping to speak with Samantha about buying me out of the Lounge."

He wrapped his arms around me from behind and continued, "We're about to have a child and I just don't think that this is the best move for us anymore. And the fact that Delilah is still a partner doesn't make things any better. So, Anthony, Beth, are either of you interested?"

"Let me call Samantha and see how she feels about it," Beth said, walking outside for some privacy. I caught both Ron and Anthony looking at her ass as she walked out. *Men.*

Nel's phone rang, too. She looked at the caller ID and smiled like she had been waiting for the call.

"Excuse me, I have to take this. Y'all sit back down and get comfortable. I'll be right back."

She walked towards the back. Even though she told us to sit down, we all stood there awkwardly, avoiding eye contact. Well, all but Anthony and Ron. Anthony looked like he wanted to jump bad with Ron. Ron just smiled like he knew something Anthony didn't. Both of women came back smiling like Cheshire cats.

"Tyrone, Sam said she'd love to buy your part of the Lounge. She offered fifteen thousand. Is that enough?" Beth said. That was the second bit of good news I'd gotten in the past hour.

"Yeah, that would be fine. We'll set up a meeting to discuss everything," Ty responded.

"No need. She's got her attorney drafting the paperwork now and we'll be in touch when they're ready. I'll get your information before I leave and we can meet at her attorney's office to finalize everything."

Ty looked down at me and I smiled at him. I was past ready to go now. But Nel didn't give us the chance to. She jumped in right when Beth finished talking.

"That's great! I have some awesome news as well. I just got the call that I've been waiting for and Shawn is now going to be managing the Urban Department of Vantech. I'll be moving to Atlanta with this handsome guy," she said looking over at Ron, "and have been given the green light to open our new branch. Shawn has been my right hand for some time now and I know that he will do a great job with marketing the Lounge for you all," she said, smiling at Shawn. I swear they've fucked.

Shawn smiled from ear-to-ear. Then Ron looked my way but I figured he was looking at Tyrone. They'd been hanging out a lot and had started doing that nonverbal communication shit that friends do. Nel saw the look, too. He looked kinda scared and that made her stop smiling and look at him with worry all over her face.

"What's up, bae?" she asked him.

"Well, first of all, congratulations to you and to Shawn. I'm happy that situation worked out. But there's one more thing that needs to be said before we close this meeting out," he said, getting down on one knee.

Nel squealed and I almost leapt out of my husband's arms. Beth even screamed in excitement.

"Nel, these last couple of months have made me happier than I could have ever imagined. You are such a strong, kind woman. You put everyone else before yourself. I know I asked you the other night and you said yes but I wanted to do this shit the right way. I asked for your hand from your brother and he gave me his blessing. Jeff gave his as well. I told you when I met you that we were gonna be the King and Queen but now we're movin' to bigger thangs and are gonna take the A by storm. Will you do me the honor of being Mrs. Blowemup?" Ron said, pulling the ring box out of his pants pocket and opening it.

Nel started crying when he put the ring on her finger. She held it up to the light. She was crying like someone had died and couldn't get anything out but sniffles.

When she finally composed herself, I got confirmation that my eerie feeling was for good reason. Delilah came walking down the stairs doin' a slow clap. That bitch was always so fuckin' dramatic. I looked and saw the gun in her sweat pants and knew shit was about to get real.

"Well... well... well... look who found her knight in shining armor. I mean, I've had the dick so I really think you're settling, Sheila," she said laughing. "Anthony is a much better fuck. But, I guess you take what you can get, huh?"

She pointed the gun at Nel and Ron shielded her with his body.

"I don't give a fuck who gets this bullet, you or her," Delilah said to Ron with a crazy look in her eyes. "Either way ain't gone be no damn wedding."

She moved the gun from one person to another like she was choosing who to shoot first.

"Y'all having this meeting without me like I'm not a partner in this business. Like you can treat me like an afterthought. Trying to get lawyers to push me outta this agreement. Y'all motherfuckas stuck with me. Or I'll just handle all of y'all and run this bitch on my own."

Tyrone slowly slid me behind him and kept his hand behind his back. I had my twenty-two in my purse and wasted no time slipping it out. I knew Ty had his on him, too and I looked over to see Beth sliding her hand into her purse that was hanging on her side. Shawn put his hands behind his back and stood wide-legged like he was standing security somewhere but I had a feeling he was strapped, too. He and Nel dealt with a lot of dope boys and rappers in their business so they stayed ready, even in their business suits and club clothes. She'd designed a garter belt that could hold her twenty-two that would let her hide it under her mini-skirt.

Delilah's ass was gonna die today. She'd fucked with all of us. Put us in danger. Fucked Nel's man while posing as her friend. Hell, fucked both of Nel's men. She'd even drugged Ron. Jumped on Nel in her own house. Shot up my house and shit. Stabbed Tanisha. Being locked up wasn't justice enough for this bitch. She had to fuckin' go!

Anthony

"Hey there beautiful?" I answered, happy to see Keisha's face pop up on my screen.

"Hey," she said, sounding shaken. My smile left my face immediately.

"You ok?"

"Naw. There was a shoot-out. The guy Tremaine... Tre who raped your business partner's wife was killed, after he raped me while I was undercover posing as his girlfriend. We got Samson, though. He's on his way to the hospital and then his ass won't see the light of day anymore," she said in one breath.

I held the phone in silence. I didn't know what to say. I didn't like any of what I'd just heard. But I knew it came with dating a cop. I tried to swallow the pill she'd just dispensed.

"Babe, you there?" she asked, my silence apparently making her feel some type of way.

"Yeah... yeah. That's just a lot to take in. You ever thought about leaving the force?"

"Actually, after today... I am. I mean, I've asked for desk duty but I really think I've had enough. If it isn't the men sexually harassing me then I have to deal with the shit from these boys who think they're men out here in these streets. The Gump ain't the place to be law enforcement."

"Let's have dinner and talk about it. My sister is at the hotel with the kids. She brought my niece and nephew so they can go swimming. I'm headed to a meeting right now at the Lounge. How about you meet me there in half an hour? We should be done by then."

"Ok. I'm gonna wash this blood off of me and go ahead and do my reports and you can follow me back to my house so I can change clothes. Is that ok?"

Blood, I thought, but I would hear about that over dinner.

"Now you know we might not make it to dinner if I follow you back to your place," I flirted trying to cheer her up. She giggled on the other end of the phone.

"Uh Unh. I will not be a cheap date tonight. Dinner *before* dessert this time, Mr. Bailey," she laughed.

I loved to hear her laugh. I was glad she was ok. I would deal with and accept everything that she'd been through because she needed me to be there for her. That's why she called me. She trusted me. It felt good to be trusted.

"I'm pullin' up, baby. I'll see you soon," I said, not really wanting to get off the phone with her.

"Ok. Love you," she said, hanging up the phone before I could respond. I loved her, too. I would be sure to tell her tonight over dinner... and dessert.

I got out the car and realized I was the first person here. I pulled out a Newport and lit it. I was gonna need it to deal with Samantha, Tyrone, and Sheila in the same room. I hoped Samantha was gonna make it. She'd called me and told me she'd been shot and Beth had saved her. I didn't know how I felt about that. I mean, as her husband, wasn't I supposed to be the one to save her? But I wasn't gonna be her husband anymore soon. I'd brought the divorce papers to serve her when she got here.

As soon as I put my square out, Sheila's assistant Shawn pulled up.

"What's up, man? Where everybody else at?" I asked as I dapped him up. Shawn and I had always been cool.

"They should be on their way. How you doin' man? You look like you gotta lot on your mind," he said as we walked up the stairs to the door of the Lounge.

"Man, keep living. You'll be walkin' around with this permanent frown, too," I laughed. "You're about to marry that beautiful fiancée of yours. You'll forever be worried about something whether it's about keeping her happy or making enough money, and don't add kids to the mix."

"Yeah, I already worry about some of that shit now," he said.

Tammy and Tyrone pulled up and were getting out of their truck right when we reached the door. Tammy looked like she was on the verge of tears but she was still fine as fuck. I had to turn my head and walk on in the house not to stare. Tyrone was one lucky man. I would've left Sam alone for a chance to be with Tammy, too. Hell, I'd leave Keisha for a chance. Keisha was fine but she wasn't Tammy fine.

I liked what I saw when I walked into the building. They had it all setup for the Grand Opening. It had a real chill feel to it. There were paintings on the wall by local artists and the furniture felt like home. I knew they'd put a bed upstairs in the VIP and a pole per my request because I already had a few strip parties lined up. I'd take Keisha up there to check that out with me when she got here.

I turned around just as Sheila walked in with that promoter nigga she's been dating. He was aight but he wasn't no me. They were hand in hand like they were in love or some shit and she had a look on her face that I knew all too well. I knew he'd just knocked her ass down before they came to the meeting. That shit pissed me off. She looked like she was tired too, though. I knew she'd been referred to the Cancer Center so I figured she was getting some kinda treatment. What kinda dude fucked a sick chick? Nigga must be desperate.

"Can we get started?" I asked, lookin' Sheila's so-called man up and down.

"We're waiting on one more person," Sheila said, not even looking at me. "Let's have a seat. She should be here shortly."

We sat down but I was mad as hell that Sheila was treating me like we never had anything special together. Then, as if shit couldn't get worse, Beth walked through the door. I was more than ready to get the hell out of here after seeing her ass. She looked like she'd lost a fight. I knew Delilah was whoopin' her ass so I didn't even blink about it. Any woman who stayed with somebody who beat the hell out of them deserved every lick, in my opinion.

"Hi..." she said, smiling and throwin' her hips. I wondered if she was putting that show on for me.

Sheila went ahead and started the meeting. She stood up and invited us all the follow her through the rest of the house as she talked. I hung back and watched the door, waiting for Samantha to come in but she didn't. I wondered if she was ok. I'd ask Beth before Keisha and I left.

"Hey Beth. Thank you for joining us today. I wanted to meet with all of you to go over the details of the Grand Opening of the Mojo Lounge next week. Shawn has the list of events and I wanted to sit down and review them together so that we can make sure that they're to your satisfaction."

Shawn handed out the folders and Tyrone started talking.

"Before you go any further, Nel, I wanna talk to Anthony and was hoping to speak with Samantha about buying me out of the Lounge."

He wrapped his arms around Tammy from behind and continued, "We're about to have a child and I just don't think that this is the best move for us anymore. And the fact that Delilah is still a partner doesn't make things any better. So, Anthony, Beth, are either of you interested?"

I smirked. I knew this nigga wasn't cut out for this shit. And now that he was tied down and married and shit, he wasn't gonna be able to hoe chase like his playboy ass thought he was going to when he signed onto the partnership in the first place.

"Let me call Samantha and see how she feels about it," Beth said, walking outside to call Sam. It rubbed me the wrong way that she was there as Sam's representative instead of me. But I watched that ass on its way out the door, though.

Sheila's phone rang, too. She looked at it and smiled, "Excuse me, I have to take this. Y'all sit back down and get comfortable. I'll be right back."

She walked towards the back. We all stood around waiting and I took the opportunity to mug the hell outta Sheila's little boyfriend. Nigga had the nerve to smile at me and shit like I wouldn't whoop his ass all over this establishment. Beth came back in first. She negotiated the deal with Tyrone that Sam had offered like she was some kinda partner and had say so and access to my wife's money.

Sheila came back in and said some shit about her and her "man" moving to Atlanta and Shawn taking over the marketing for the Lounge, which I was cool with because I knew the young nigga was on his shit. Then her man got down on one knee and I felt myself about to blow.

Sheila squealed like she had been waiting for this nigga to ask her to marry him or something. Beth screamed and Tammy grinned all wide.

"Nel, these last couple of months have made me happier than I could have ever imagined. You are such a strong, kind woman. You put everyone else before yourself. I know I asked you the other night and you said yes but I wanted to do this shit the right way. I asked for your hand from your brother and he gave me his blessing. Jeff gave his as well. I told you when I met you that we were gonna be the King and Queen but now we're movin' to bigger thangs and are gonna take the A by storm. Will you do me the honor of being Mrs. Blowemup?" he said, pulling the ring box out of his pants pocket and opening it.

Sheila put on a show with the tears and shit but I caught her glimpse at me one good time in the process. Then I heard clapping and looked up to see Delilah walking down the stairs with a gun in her pants doing the hater's signature slow clap.

"Well... well... well... look who found her knight in shining armor. I mean, I've had the dick so I really think you're settling, Sheila," she said laughing. "Anthony is a much better fuck. But, I guess you take what you can get, huh?"

I looked at the nigga and smiled like 'yeah, you heard her. My dick was better'.

She pulled out her gun and pointed it at Sheila. When her man blocked Delilah's shot, she went on a rant before pointing the gun at each of us. I didn't hear a word she said. All I could think about was all the shit I'd done to the women in my life and this crazy ass bitch was gonna kill me right when I found somebody I felt like I could have a chance with. I knew some shit was about to go down because I saw Tammy and Beth both reach in their purses and Sheila pull up her man's shirt from behind him. I started looking around for the best place to duck for cover. Not one motherfucker in here was worth me dying for.

Samantha

I was laying on the couch with ripped towels wrapped around my right leg as tourniquets and dried blood all around my knee when the sun shone through the blinds into my eyes. I'd lost so much blood that I was in and out but when I opened my eyes all the way, I saw Beth standing over me. I thought I was hallucinating at first but, when she didn't disappear when I blinked a few times, I knew she was really there. I smiled at her because she was risking her life to save mine. I didn't know how she'd gotten into the house and didn't care. I just wanted the both of us outta there as soon as damn possible.

"Come on, baby. I gotta get you outta here," she said, and leaned down to help me up.

"I can't walk, Beth. This shit hurts so bad. Them pain pills they gave me ain't doin' shit for this pain," I was barely able to get out.

"So we gotta get you outta here and to the hospital. Come on, baby. You can do this," she said, not giving up. I loved that about her. If she was nothing else, she was relentless.

I looked at her sadly before laying back on the couch. I couldn't get up. I just wanted to lay there and die and for her to get to safety. She started crying uncontrollably.

"Sam, I'm not gonna leave you here for these crazy motherfuckers to hurt you anymore! Now get the hell up and let's go get you some help!" she screamed at me.

She didn't see Samson come in the house. My eyes got wide as he grabbed a handful of her hair and snatched her backwards with a smile on his face. It pissed me off. I mustered up the strength to sit up. I wasn't gonna let him hurt her.

"Let her go, Samson," I said, angrily.

"Ohhhh, this is your little girlfriend, huh? Delilah told me she had your nose wide the fuck open. We're only as strong as the thing we're weak for. So, let's see how strong you are, Samantha," he said, and I knew what he was about to do. "Beth, you're gonna determine whether or not you and Samantha get outta here alive or whether you're gonna die together."

"Samson, *don't! Please!*" I said, tears running down my cheeks.

"Shut up or I'll make you watch," he spat at me. I laid back down on the couch, defeated.

"It's ok, baby. You know I'll do anything for you. Just promise me you'll still love me and want me when we get outta here," Beth said and I felt sick to my stomach.

I nodded to Beth and she mouthed the words 'I love you' before I turned away. I couldn't watch him drag her down the hallway to have his way with her.

They were back there for what felt like forever. I had cried myself tearless hearing him fuck her. When Delilah walked into the house, I just knew the shit was about to hit the fan. She was gonna go the fuck off when she walked back there and saw Samson fuckin' Beth. To my surprise, she came storming back through the apartment shortly after and was out the door. She was mad as fuck but it looked like her fear of Samson had curbed her crazy.

Beth came back up front and grabbed me, dragging me to her car. She laid me across her back seat. I couldn't look at her. I knew that she'd made the sacrifice for me but it didn't take away from the fact of what had happened. She drove to Baptist East without saying a word, but she kept her eyes on me through the rearview mirror. Finally, when she came to get me out of the car to help me into the wheelchair that the ER attendant had brought, I looked at her. She still had scars that were healing from Delilah beating her up. She'd just given her body to a man to save our lives. She deserved better from me.

"I love you Elizabeth," I said, smiling at her then groaning because my damn leg was killing me.

She didn't say anything back but her eyes said enough.

*****

Now here I was laid up in this hospital bed with my leg elevated. I'd just gotten a shot in my knee and now I had a morphine pump. I was feeling good, waiting for the cops to get here so I could give my statement on what happened. Beth didn't wanna leave me but I needed her to go to that meeting at the Lounge so I knew what was going on. Sheila offered to stop by the hospital once I told her I'd been shot. I told her that Beth would be coming in my stead and she accepted. I was just about to doze off when my phone rang.

"Hey baby," I said nearly out of it.

"Hey darlin'. How you feelin'?"

"I'm floatin' right now so I'm good."

She giggled at me but then her tone turned serious.

"Baby, I think I saw Delilah's car parked a couple blocks up from the Lounge on the way here. I think she might be here or close by."

"You got your protection?" I asked, instantly becoming alert.

"Always. You know I don't leave home without it nowadays."

"Alright, be careful. I need you to come back to me in one piece," I said sweetly into the phone.

"You know I'm coming back to you, Sam. No worries. Oh, and the reason I called you. I walked into the meeting just in time for Tyrone to say he wanted to sell out of his share of the Lounge. He wanted to give you and Anthony the opportunity to buy him out."

"Oh really? Ok. Offer him fifteen thousand. The max we'll pay for it is forty-five, though. I'll call my lawyer and get them started on the paperwork," I said, knowing she was gonna handle that shit for me.

"Ok. I got you, baby. See you soon."

"Look," I said before she hung up, "if you see that bitch Delilah, shoot first and ask questions later, you hear me? She doesn't value life. And you know she's gunnin' for you just as bad as she is those other motherfuckers in there, especially after this morning," I said, getting frustrated thinking about that shit again.

"Ok baby, love you," she said.

"Love you, too. Be safe."

I hung up the phone just as the cops were coming into the room to take my statement. There were two of them, both male, one was fine as hell and I remembered him from when Tyrone's house had been vandalized. The other was a handsome young white cop with pale blue eyes that looked like water and light brown hair. I wouldn't mind letting either of them cuff me and lay down the law.

I debated telling them what Beth had just told me but decided against it. We'd given them enough chances to get Delilah's ass. Now it was time to take matters into our own hands. I knew one of them was gonna take her ass out. I would call my lawyer as soon as the police officers left to get the paperwork drawn up to purchase Tyrone's share of the Lounge.

"Ms. Johnson, how are you feeling?" the white male officer asked.

"As well as can be expected seeing that I've been shot," I answered sarcastically. He looked like I'd hurt his feelings.

His partner laughed aloud, "Ms. Johnson, I'm sure you remember me. We know you're angry and frustrated by everything that's happening right now so we'll make this quick."

"That would be much appreciated," I said, sucking my teeth. I was ready for them to get the hell on. I pushed my morphine button, I was starting to feel the pain in my leg again.

"Can you tell us what happened?" the white officer asked.

"Yeah. I came home from a trip with my girlfriend and Delilah Powell, my sister and former nanny and my husband's former mistress, was waiting for me in my house."

"How did she get in?" he interrupted me.

"She broke in and used the code to disarm the alarm," I said, rolling my eyes.

"How did she know the code?" he asked.

"Look man, catch your slow ass partner up, please," I said, getting tired of the dumb ass questions.

"Ma'am, I'm just tryin' to get facts. It's not every day that I hear that a woman who I assumed you fired from watching your children, I assume because you caught her sleeping with your husband, would still know the code to your alarm. Most people would have the mental wherewithal to change their code," he said, looking like he'd had enough of my attitude.

"Jon, I got this," his partner said, unable to hide his laughter. "Why don't you go get some coffee?"

Jon cut his eyes at me one more good time before he left.

"I see why somebody would wanna shoot her ass," he said under his breath loud enough for me to hear before he walked out the room.

"So you were saying Miss Powell was waiting for you when you got home. What happened next?" the black officer asked.

"She shot me and kidnapped me. Took me to my girlfriend, Beth's apartment where she'd been hiding out with our biological father. Samson…"

"Samson Powell? We have him in custody. Ok. So, what happened after that?" I could tell he was ready to go in search of some coffee himself by the way he was rushing me.

"Samson tied towels around my leg and gave me a pain pill. I passed out from the pain. When I woke up, Beth was there trying to get me out of the house. I don't know how she got in there but yeah, she was trying to get me outta there when Samson came back in the house. I don't even remember him leaving. But anyway, he made her have sex with him to save our lives. And then he let us go. But not before Delilah came in and caught them having sex and stormed out."

"Why would she storm out?" he asked, obviously interested in the story now.

"Because she's been sleeping with Samson."

"Didn't you say he was both of your father?" he looked confused and then disgusted when he figured out what was going on.

"There you go! Now you got it," I shook my head. No wonder Delilah's ass was still free. These cops 'round here were remedial as hell.

"Ok," he said, clearing his throat like that would make my story any easier to digest. "Then what happened?"

"Beth came back and got me and brought me here."

"Ok. I think I have everything I need. I'm gonna let you rest. I hope you're able to regain full mobility," he said, turning to walk out of the room.

"Sir, you said Samson is in custody. Please don't let him get out. He's a dangerous person."

"Oh he won't. He's gonna get life for the informant he murdered when we apprehended him," he said, walking out of the room.

I laid back, deciding to rest and call my attorney later. I dozed off for what felt like hours but, when I looked at the clock had only been a half hour and I looked at my phone to see if I had any missed calls. I was starting to worry about Beth because I hadn't heard anything from her. I hadn't heard anything from Kris either and I was sure he would have called me pissed that Beth was handling my business for me. I decided to call her to make sure everything was copacetic.

"Hello," she answered, sounding out of breath.

"You ok?"

"Yeah. She's dead baby. She won't bother any of us anymore," she said.

"What happened?"

"The less you know the better. Just know she's in a body bag. I gotta go, baby. The cops are questioning us. I'll be up there as soon as I can."

I felt my blood pressure going up. I paged the nurse. I swear between Kris, Beth, Delilah, and my children, they were all trying to kill me. At least I had one less of them to worry about now.

Delilah

"Well... well... well... look who found her knight in shining armor. I mean, I've had the dick so I really think you're settling, Sheila," I laughed, pulling my gun out of my pants. "Anthony is a much better fuck. But, I guess you take what you can get, huh?"

I pointed the gun at her but her nigga wanted to play Captain Save-A-Hoe and blocked my shot with his body. I would just shoot his ass in the head and then she'd be mine.

I stood there, waving the gun from one to the next, enjoying the fear that I was instilling in their hearts. I had all of their asses where I wanted them and was gonna take them out one by one. I wanted Sheila's ass first but fuck that, I was gonna make her watch as everyone she loved was gunned down. I was finally gonna win.

"I don't give a fuck who gets this bullet, you or her," she said to me. "Either way ain't gone be no damn wedding," I said, playing duck-duck-goose with them, the nozzle of the gun the deciding factor in the game.

"Y'all having this meeting without me like I'm not a partner in this business. Like you can treat me like an afterthought. Trying to get lawyers to push me outta this agreement. Y'all motherfuckas stuck with me. Or I'll just handle all of y'all and run this bitch on my own."

I was livid. I knew that there was no way that the Lounge would happen without them. I knew that I was probably gonna have to leave town. After all the shit I'd done, Samson and I would be on the run for a while. But that would give us the chance to start over. Maybe we could go to a nice non-extradition island and be together and in love. Maybe then he'd only have eyes for me.

In my daydreaming, I didn't see Sheila pull out a gun. I didn't know where the bitch got it from. But she wasn't as fast as I was. She pulled out and I shot in the air, making her ass duck and fall to the floor. I fired another shot into the wall by her head to show her I wasn't fuckin' playin'.

"Do you think this is a fuckin' game? Bitch, I've been wanting to shoot yo' punk ass from the moment I met you. You're weak. A waste. You think you have power 'cause some white motherfuckers respect you but you're nothing more than a token to meet their Equal Opportunity quota. I was gonna make you watch but now I'm gonna take your ass out of your misery first," I yelled, aiming the gun directly at her head this time.

There was no way I could have seen what was coming. Here I thought I had these motherfuckers under control. My cockiness got the best of me and I felt something that could only be described as fire through my chest, leg, and ear. I lost control of my body and fell to the floor. The pain was unbelievable. I started coughing and knew I'd been shot. I could barely breathe and looked up and they were all standing over me. I knew I wasn't gonna make it out of here alive because none of them had out their phones out calling for an ambulance. They were gonna watch the life leave my body. Beth, Tammy, Shawn, and Sheila had their guns drawn like they were all ready to fire more shots into my body if I decided to move.

My vision was going in and out and then I heard someone yell, "Police!"

Before I could see who'd come in, they all put their weapons away. I laughed because, I was gonna use my last breath to get the last laugh. They all turned to look at the cop, but no one moved. Then they looked back down at me.

"What the hell happened in here?" she asked as she walked closer.

I was struggling to breathe and the coughs were becoming more violent.

"Stand clear," she said as she gave me CPR. Everyone stepped back. I looked at her, letting know I wanted to say something. She leaned in and I whispered in her ear, "Sheila shot me. He's got her gun."

I started laughing and felt the pain grow unbearable, but I refused to cry. Coughing up more blood, I saw darkness before the pain stopped and I took what I knew was my last breath.

This was *so* not how this shit was supposed to go. Where was my happy ending? My happily ever after? Everything I did and I still lost to Sheila's ass. But before it was all over, I made sure that bitch was goin' down. Her life would be over when she was convicted of my murder.

Epilogue

Sheila

When it rains it pours. All of my dreams were coming true when Ron proposed to me and then that lunatic Delilah comes and crashes the party. I was so glad to see her ass laying in a pool of blood on the floor. It felt like a weight had been lifted off my shoulders. Until...

"Police!" I heard a woman yell.

We all hid our guns before she'd gotten all the way in the building. As soon as we'd heard the word police, we knew we had to get them outta sight. I felt the breath catch in my throat as we all turned around to look at the officer who was standing there with her gun drawn. She looked at us all, her gaze with Anthony lingering, and then down at Delilah. Nobody moved. We hadn't called the cops so I was baffled by her presence.

All of our gazes travelled back to Delilah laying there, coughing up blood, on the floor. I looked around at everyone because I figured we were all going Downtown. Anthony looked like he was about to pass out. Tyrone had his arms wrapped around Tammy who was staring blankly at Delilah. It was like she pitied her but was just as glad as I was that she was dead. Beth looked like she wanted to cry. She'd actually had some kinda love for Delilah's crazy ass. Shawn was looking at me, waiting for instructions. His eyes told me he was willing to take responsibility for the shooting but I couldn't do that to him. Ron squeezed my hand, making me break my gaze with Shawn and gave me a reassuring look. I loved him so much.

I let out a breath while staring into his eyes and realized that I hadn't been breathing all that time.

"What the hell happened in here?" the Officer asked as she walked closer to the body.

Delilah was heaving and spitting up blood. I knew she was about to die. None of us answered. She looked at Anthony again, like she expected him to speak up and answer her question. He just looked away.

"Stand clear," she said as she gave Delilah CPR. Everyone stepped back.

Delilah looked at her like she wanted to say something to her. She leaned in and my heart skipped a beat. She whispered in her ear before laughing and coughing up more blood. Then she took her last breath.

The cop got up and ran out the door. When she got back into the building, we all looked like we were waiting for her to say something. I expected her to read us our rights. Instead she looked at each of us, one by one, then down at Delilah with the gun in her hand, and shook her head.

"Listen. If any of you have a weapon, I need you to take that shit to your car. Go wash your hands, too. I called for backup so they're on their way," she said.

We all looked at her like she was crazy.

"MOVE!" she yelled and we all scattered. We went to our cars to put our guns in the glove boxes. Anthony didn't move. He didn't have a weapon.

"Baby, you think this is a setup?" I asked Ron as we walked back into the building.

"Only one way to find out," he shrugged.

We went back in and she was squatted beside Delilah's body like she was figuring something out. We stood over her, waiting for the next set of instructions.

"Listen," she said, "here's what's gonna happen. You're gonna tell your version of what happened in here up until Delilah was shot. Then you're gonna say I came in and shot her. You got me?"

We all nodded at her but were looking at her in disbelief. *Who the fuck is this woman and why is she willing to take the wrap for us?* I asked myself.

"You ok, baby?" she asked Anthony and I put two and two together. Leave it to this nigga to be fuckin' a cop.

"Yeah. Yeah," he said, looking shaken. "You sure you wanna do this?" he asked her.

"Yeah, I'm sure. There were lots of people who wanted Delilah dead and I know a great deal of what she put y'all through. Y'all have children and shit that you need to be free for or I'll be locking their asses up in the future mad as hell because I could have prevented it. So let me do this so y'all can go on with your lives, ok?"

Everyone nodded in unison.

"Now, I need everyone's information. Business cards with your personal numbers on them in case some shit hits the fan. Hopefully, you won't ever have to hear from me. But I want to have direct access to y'all just in case," she instructed and we all gave her our information. Hell, I didn't wanna hear from her ass anymore, either.

When her backup arrived, they interviewed us all. I watched as they wheeled Delilah out of the house with a white sheet over her body and put her in the coroner's van. I couldn't believe that a woman that I had considered a friend had put me and my family through so much. You have to be careful who you fuck with. You never know what they may be capable of.

Out of the corner of my eye, I saw Beth walk away from the Officer she was talking to and answer a call. She walked back over shortly after and finished talking to him.

Mr. Hussein, the owner of the property, pulled up in a Honda Sonata and hopped out of his car.

"What's going on?" he asked, seeming concerned.

"Sir, I need you to stay behind the tape," I heard an officer tell him.

"This is my property and I need to know what's happening," he argued.

Anthony's girlfriend walked over to him and said something. I guess she was trying to calm him down.

"Taken down? As in killed? Someone was killed in my building? I'm calling my attorney. The lease is *terminated*. Tell whoever has their shit in there that I want it out by the end of the day!" I heard him yell, pulling out his phone and stomping away.

I looked at Shawn and we knew that we had to handle business. He and I walked over to Mr. Hussein together.

"Mr. Hussein, I'm Sheila Price with Vantech Marketing and this is my Assistant, Shawn, remember us?" I asked because we had met with him several times when Delilah was locked up.

"Yes. Yes, I do. Your lease will be terminated in the morning. I am having my attorney draw up the papers," he said, his phone still to his ear.

"Mr. Hussein, you may want to reconsider that for two reasons. First, you won't be able to sell or rent this property for anywhere *near* what it's worth now that there's been someone killed in there," I pointed out, and he lowered his phone.

"And secondly," Shawn picked up where I left off, "our lease says that there has to be some illegal activity that has taken place on the property in order for you to terminate the lease without penalty. Now, as you will see in the police report that I will provide you, the death that occurred in the building was a good shoot by a Montgomery Police Officer with an impeccable record. There was no illegal activity on the premises. Even the deceased's gun was registered to her. Now, if you want to take your chances in court, where I'm sure your attorney will tell you that it will be a loss, have at it. We'll happily let you resume your conversation with your attorney and go ahead and call ours as well."

I smirked at Shawn. All those late nights in the office when we were fuckin' had paid off. He'd learned more than how this pussy gripped. If I wasn't engaged and in love with Ron, I'd tell his ass to meet mw back at the office and rock his ass 'til his toes curled for the way he just handled that. He looked at me and smiled like he was reading my mind.

Mr. Hussein placed the phone back to his ear and his attorney must have said something similar because he looked at us with a wrinkled forehead.

"Meet me at my office tomorrow at ten," he said. "The lease cannot be in the name of a deceased person."

"We'll get in touch with Mr. Bailey and Mrs. Johnson. They've agreed to assume full responsibility for the lease, and see you then," Shawn said, extending his hand. Mr. Hussein shook it and got back into his car and pulled away. I was so glad Shawn was taking over this project and Sam was buying Tyrone out. My brother and I never had to deal with either Samantha or Tyrone ever again.

When we walked back to the Lounge, Anthony's girlfriend gave me an impressed look. I gave her a quick wink and went back to Ron's side while he gave his statement.

*****

We walked away in the clear. I was ready to get the hell out of the Gump as soon as humanly fuckin' possible. We were on our way to get Jeff when my phone rang.

"Hello," I answered it without looking at the caller ID.

"Nel, come get me the hell up outta here. They just gave me my freedom papers," Tanisha said, laughter in her voice.

I couldn't do anything but shake my head. I was glad that she was ok but that woman was a damn character.

"Yes, ma'am," I said laughing. "We'll be there in a just a minute."

"Goin' to get Tanisha?" Ron asked, changing his route.

"Mmm hmmm," I nodded my head. Secretly I was hoping she didn't need any care that would require her moving in with me because I was about to start packing my shit as soon as I got home.

When we got to the hospital, Tanisha was standing outside, smoking a cigarette. Her ass didn't care that it was a smoke-free campus. I heard Ron laugh under his breath and all I could do was roll my eyes. She got in the car with a thud, not even putting her cigarette out. I rolled down her window.

"Where we taking you to, Ma?" I asked.

"Home. I ain't gone burden y'all with having to take care of me. They said they'll send a home health worker to take care of me so I'll be fine."

"You sure?" I asked, not really wanting her to change her answer.

"Yeah, I'm sure. I gotta hurry up and get better so I can come visit y'all in Atlanta and help take care of my new grandbaby that's on the way," she said.

I looked back at her in awe. I knew Ty had told her everything before we got there. He couldn't hold good news worth a shit.

"And it sounds like I gotta wedding to help plan, too," she said, grinning at Ron in the rearview mirror.

"Yes, ma'am," he smiled back.

"Show me that rock, girl," she said to me, hitting the back of the seat.

I held my hand up so she could see the ring. I was proud to be the future Mrs. Ronald Roberts.

"Oooh wee! Boy, you dropped the down payment on a house on her finger, huh?" she said, then reached down and grabbed her side like it hurt.

"She's worth every penny," Ron said, reaching out and taking my hand.

"I hope that crazy bitch Delilah don't come trying to crash the wedding."

"She's dead, Mama," I said, surprised that Tyrone had left that little tidbit out.

"Dead? Rest in Peace, Honey. But I'm glad that bitch is gone. God forgive me for speaking ill of the dead but he knew he made a rotten one when he created that child there," she said.

"Mama, you so damn country," I laughed.

We pulled up to her apartment complex and she sat for a second, a sadness coming over her.

"Samson dead, too?" she asked.

"No ma'am. He's in jail. He'll be dead before he get outta there, though," I shared with her what Keisha, Anthony's girlfriend, had told me.

She let out a heavy sigh.

"I loved that man. Loved him so much I let him ruin me. I gotta second chance at life. I'm gonna appreciate every moment of it," she said, flicking her cigarette butt out of the window.

She opened the door and got out of the car.

"Mama, you got more damn lives than a cat," I said, leaning out of the window to kiss her. "Call me if you need anything. And I do mean *anything*," I said. We watched her walk into her apartment and pulled off to pick up our son, ready to move on with our lives.

Beth

Six months later

I sat in the living room, my face full of tears. I knew Kris would be bringing the kids home soon so I needed to start dinner, but I couldn't make myself get up. I'd gone to the clinic after Samson forced me to have sex with him to make sure he hadn't given me anything. I'd come back negative for everything the first time but, because they'd said it could take anywhere from six months to three years for HIV or AIDS to show up. I'd gone back monthly as a precaution. Sam and I had even been using dental dam to protect ourselves. Never in a million years would I have thought that I would have actually contracted something.

I stared at the piece of paper. The words "POSITIVE" stared back at me. I wanted to take my life. I didn't want to die a slow and painful death but I knew I had to at least tell Samantha what was going on. I picked up my phone.

"Hey there, beautiful," she said, sounding like she was in a good mood. I hated to be the one to ruin it.

"Hey," I sniffled.

"Awww baby, what's wrong?"

"I got my results back and I've got AIDS."

The line got quiet. I wanted her to say something comforting. I needed her to tell me that it was gonna be ok. And she just sat there holding the phone, saying nothing.

"Sam?"

"Yeah, I'm here."

"Say something!"

"I don't know what to say, baby. You definitely didn't get it from me. We can assume that either Samson or Delilah gave it to you," she rationalized.

"No shit!" I said, angry that she was stating the obvious.

"Don't get mad with me. Hell, now I need to get tested. Look, let's talk when I get home. We'll get through this together. You saved my life. I'm not gonna abandon you. I just gotta process this, ok? We'll talk when I get home," she repeated.

I hung up the phone and cried harder than I had when I received the paper. The nurse said that I could live a normal life as long as I took my meds and gave me the information for a support group. I didn't want this to be real. But there was nothing I could do about it now. I got up and put the pasta in a pot and turned it on to boil. I wasn't gonna let this diagnosis end my life. And as long as I had Samantha by my side, my life, what was left of it, would be a happy one.

Tammy

"Ty! Come on! We're gonna be late!" I yelled as I rubbed the perfume on my wrists. He got on my nerves. He knew it was gonna take me forever to get anywhere with this big ass boy I was carrying and I didn't want to miss Imani on stage.

"Woman, I told you I was coming," Tyrone said, grinning and wrapping his arms around my huge belly from behind.

I rolled my eyes at him in the mirror. He looked so good in his powder blue Polo shirt. His locs were freshly styled. And he smelled like Dolce & Gabbana. I almost forgot that I wanted to go somewhere and let my pregnant sex drive get the best of me.

"You better back up before I try to climb my big ass on top of you," I smirked at his reflection.

"No you won't, either. I ain't tryna get squashed," he said, laughing. "But I'll bend that juicy ass over, though," he said, taking the opportunity to pull up my skirt and move my panties to the side.

He started kissing on my neck and my eyes rolled back in my head.

"Baby, we gotta go," I argued, not stopping him as I felt him unbuttoning his pants and heard his belt buckle clatter on our hardwood floor.

He bent me over my vanity and slid into me. He felt so good I screamed his name with every stroke. He held onto my hips and worked my g-spot, making me cum all over him and down my legs.

"Tyrone! Oh my *GOD*! I love you. Right there, baby! Right there! Shit," I said, shuddering and cumming again.

"Oh *shit* this pussy wet as hell. I'mma keep yo' ass pregnant, I swear!" he said and I felt his dick throb as he came inside of me.

He kissed me between my shoulder blades and I pulled my skirt down. We walked into the bathroom to wash up.

"This baby gone be born with a dent in his forehead," I joked as I washed the cum from my thighs and calves.

"We'll call it a birthmark," he laughed and I laughed with him because we both knew that made no damn sense. "Now come on, you're gonna make us late," he said, smacking me on the ass and walking out of the bathroom.

I gave his back a death stare but stepped out of my panties, went to my dresser and put on a new pair, and waddled my ass out the door.

When we pulled up to Montini's, the parking lot was packed.

"See, now we ain't gone have no damn seat! Imani told us to get here early," I fussed.

"Your pregnant ass can always get a seat. Now, come on here and hush," he said, helping me out of the car.

We walked up to the door and saw Imani sitting at a table. She'd held our seats. She looked beautiful with her huge Afro combed to one side. She had on a form-fitting camouflage cat suit that showed off her slim thickness and a pair of chocolate brown thigh-high boots.

The show hadn't started yet. The DJ was playing *Phone Down* from Erykah Badu's *But You Caint Use My Phone* Mixtape. We made our way across the room to my new friend. With Nel gone, Imani and I had gotten really close.

"Heyyyy belly!" she greeted me, standing up and kissing me on the cheek.

"Hey there, goddess," I replied as she and Tyrone hugged. I thought I saw a look between them but I blew it off. They were just really cool. Ty appreciated that Imani went with me to the doctor when he was stuck at work.

"I'm going to get a drink. Y'all want anything?" Tyrone asked after helping me into my seat.

"Cranberry juice for me, please baby," I said.

"Naw. I got my Hypnotq Martini already, Ty. But thank you," Imani said, sipping the blue liquid from her glass.

"Good evening Groovers!" the hostess said, walking up to the mic. "Are y'all ready for some poetry?"

"Yeah," the crowd responded.

"Well, my name is Phoenix for those newcomers to Poetic Grooves. And I'll be your hostess for the evening. So just sit back, relax, and enjoy the edu-tainment. Oh," she said, smiling and raising her martini glass, "and don't forget to go pay that fine piece of man Mike behind the bar a visit."

Tyrone came back with my cranberry juice and some Cognac in a glass for himself. He sat down and grabbed my hand, his eyes glued to the stage. You never would have known that I had almost had to beg his ass to come with me the way he was acting. I'd been to the show a few times and knew he would enjoy it. Plus, it was something different than our usual dinner date night.

"Let's get this show started!" she said, looking at her clipboard. "First to the stage, y'all give it up for Miss Not In Love Jones!"

I yelled and clapped loudly as Imani got up and made her way to the stage. Baby Ty seemed to be clapping for her too, the way he was flopping around in my stomach. I knew I wasn't gonna make it the entire show with all the noise and loud music so I was glad Imani was going first. Tyrone placed his hand on my belly and that calmed the baby down almost instantly. I looked at him lovingly. I loved the father-son bond they had already.

"Heyyyy y'all!" Imani greeted the crowd.

"Heyyyy Miss Jones," they responded.

"I ain't gonna keep y'all long. I got one piece for y'all tonight. It's called *A Good Girl with Bad Habits*..."

The End!
Of this story, at least. Lol. Check out the spin-off, Magnum and
Bussa, Above The Law. Available Now!

About the Author

Joi Miner, 38, is a mother of two beautiful daughters from Montgomery, AL (currently residing in Birmingham, AL). She is a full-time author, editor, performance poet, storyteller, sexual assault and domestic violence activist, and entrepreneur, who loves spending time with her family, hosting shows, and listening to good music. She enjoys writing engaging stories, with plot twists that keep readers on their seats! As a freelance non-fiction contributor, for her personal blog, as well as well-known blog sites such as Negus Who Read and I Am The F-Bomb, she shares her insights into this crazy world we live in.

I'd Love to Hear from You!

Here's how to find me:

[My Blog] My Life Is A Joi Miner Novel: www.mylifeisajoiminernovel.com

Email: authorjoiminer@gmail.com

Twitter: @joiminer

Instagram: joiminer

Facebook: https://www.facebook.com/joiminer

Facebook Overflow Profile: https://www.facebook.com/authorjoiminer

Author Page: https://www.facebook.com/joiminer2

Subscribe to my Newsletter: http://eepurl.com/cKJ7bf

www.ingramcontent.com/pod-product-compliance
Lightning Source LLC
Chambersburg PA
CBHW070922130626
46555CB00001B/239